Miss Daisy Is Crazy!

and other stories

Miss Daisy Is Crazy!

and other stories

Dan Gutman

Pictures by
Jim Paillot

HarperTrophy®
An Imprint of HarperCollinsPublishers

ISBN-13: 978-0-06-209153-6
Manufactured 04/12
Manufactured in the United States.
12 LP/BR 10 9 8 7 6 5 4 3 2

My Weird School #1

Miss Daisy Is Crazy!

Dan Gutman

Pictures by Jim Paillot

HarperTrophy®
An Imprint of HarperCollinsPublishers

To Emma

I Hate School!

"My name is A.J. I like football and video games, and I hate school." Our teacher, Miss Daisy, was taking attendance. It was the first day of second grade. Miss Daisy told everyone in the class to stand up, say our name, and say something about ourself.

1

All the kids laughed when I said I hated school. But there was nothing funny about it. I have learned a lot in my eight years. One thing I learned is that there is no reason why kids should have to go to school.

If you ask me, kids can learn all we need to learn by watching TV. You can learn important information like which breakfast cereal tastes best and what toys you should buy and which shampoo leaves your hair the shiniest. This is stuff that we'll need to know when we grow up.

School is just this dumb thing that grown-ups thought up so they wouldn't have to pay for baby-sitters. When I grow up and have children of my own, I won't make them go to school. They can just ride their bikes and play football and video games all day. They'll be happy, and they'll think I'm the greatest father in the world.

But for now, I wanted to let my new teacher, Miss Daisy, know from the very start how I felt about school.

"You know what, A.J.?" Miss Daisy said, "I hate school too."

"You do?"

We all stared at Miss Daisy. I thought teachers loved school. If they didn't love school, why did they become teachers?

Why would they ever want to go to a school as a grown-up? I know that when I'm a grown-up, I'm not going to go anywhere near a school.

"Sure I hate school," Miss Daisy continued. "If I didn't have to be here teaching you, I could be home sitting on my comfortable couch, watching TV and eating bonbons."

"Wow!" we all said.

"What's a bonbon?" asked Ryan, a kid with black sneakers who was sitting next to me.

"Bonbons are these wonderful chocolate treats," Miss Daisy told us. "They're about the size of a large acorn, and you can pop the whole thing right in your mouth so you don't need a napkin. I could eat a whole box of bonbons in one sitting."

"They sound delicious!" said Andrea Young, a girl with curly brown hair. She was sitting up real straight in the front of the class with her hands folded like they were attached to each other.

Miss Daisy seemed like a pretty cool lady, for a teacher. Anybody who hated school and liked to sit around watching TV and eating chocolate treats was okay by me.

Me and Miss Daisy had a lot in common. Maybe going to school wouldn't be so terrible after all.

Dumb
Miss Daisy
and
Principal Klutz

2

Miss Daisy said it was time for us to clear off our desks and see how much we knew about arithmetic.

Ugh!

"If I gave you fifty-eight apples and Principal Klutz took twenty-eight of them away," Miss Daisy asked, "how many apples would you have left? A.J.?"

"Who cares how many apples you would have left?" I said. "I hate apples. If you ask me, you and Principal Klutz can take all the apples away and it wouldn't bother me one bit."

"You would have thirty apples," said that girl Andrea Young in the front of the class. She had a big smile on her face, like she had just opened all her birthday presents. Andrea Young thinks she's so smart.

"I hate arithmetic," I announced.

"You know what?" Miss Daisy said. "I hate arithmetic too!"

"You do?" we all said.

"Sure! I don't even know

what you get if
you multiply four
times four."

"You don't?"

"I have no idea,"
Miss Daisy said, scratch-
ing her head and wrinkling up her forehead like she was trying to figure it out.
"Maybe one of you kids can explain it to
me?"

Boy, Miss Daisy was really dumb! Even I know what you get when you multiply four times four. But that smarty-pants-I-know-everything-girl Andrea Young beat me to it and got called on first.

"If you put four crayons in a row," she told Miss Daisy as she put a bunch of crayons on the top of her desk, "and you make four rows of four crayons, you'll have sixteen crayons. See?" Then she counted the crayons from one to sixteen.

Miss Daisy looked at the crayons on Andrea's desk. She

had a puzzled look on her face.

"I'm not sure I understand," she said. "Can somebody else explain it to me?"

Michael Robinson, this kid wearing a red T-shirt with a dirt bike on it, explained four times four again, using pencils. He had sixteen pencils on his desk, in four rows of four pencils. Miss Daisy still had a look on her face like she didn't understand.

"What would happen if you subtracted half of the pencils?" she asked.

Michael took away two of the rows of pencils and put them in his pencil box.

"Then you would have eight pencils!"

we all said.

Andrea Young added, "Half of sixteen is eight."

Miss Daisy wrinkled up her forehead until it was almost like an accordion. She still didn't get it!

She started counting the pencils on Michael's desk out loud and using her fingers. She got it all wrong. We gathered around Michael's desk and tried to explain to Miss Daisy how to add, subtract, multiply, and divide numbers using the pencils.

Nothing worked. Miss Daisy had to be the dumbest teacher in the history of the world! No matter how many times we tried to explain, she kept shaking her head.

"I'm sorry," she said. "It will take me a while to understand arithmetic. Maybe you can explain it to me more tomorrow. For now we have to clean off our desks because Principal Klutz is going to come in and talk to us."

I know all about principals. My friend Billy from around the corner, who was in second grade last year, told me that the principal is like the king of the school. He runs everything.

Billy says that if you break the rules, you have to go to the principal's office, which is in a dungeon down in the basement. Kids in the dungeon get locked up and are forced to listen to their parents' old CDs for hours. It must be horrible.

Miss Daisy told us to be on our best behavior so Principal Klutz would see how mature we were. Finally he walked into our room.

"Welcome to the second grade," he said cheerfully. "I'm sure we are all going to have a wonderful year together."

Principal Klutz said a lot of stuff about the rules of the school. We're not allowed to run in the halls, and we're not allowed to chew gum. Stuff like that.

But I wasn't listening very closely

because I kept staring at his head. He had no hair at all! I mean none! His head looked like a giant egg.

When Principal Klutz was all done telling us the rules of the school, he asked if anybody had any questions about what he had said.

"Did all your hair fall out of your head," I asked, "or did you cut it off?" Everybody laughed, even though I didn't say anything funny. Miss Daisy looked at me with a mean face.

"Actually, it was both," Principal Klutz

replied with a chuckle. "Almost all of my hair fell out on its own, so I decided to shave the rest of it off."

"That's the saddest story I ever heard!" said this girl named Emily, and she burst into tears.

"Don't feel bad," Principal Klutz said. "It could have been a lot worse."

"How?" sniffled Emily.

"Well, at least my brain didn't fall out of my head!"

We all laughed, even Emily. Principal Klutz was a pretty funny guy, for a principal.

"Any other questions?"

"Do you have a dungeon down in the

basement where you put the bad kids?" I asked.

"Actually, the dungeon is on the third floor," Principal Klutz replied.

Nobody laughed this time. He quickly told us that he was just making a joke and that he didn't even have a dungeon at all.

Principal Klutz must have felt bad that we didn't think his joke was funny, because he invited us all up to the front of the room to touch his bald head.

We did, and that made everybody feel a lot better.

Principal Klutz seemed nice, but a lot of people seem nice when you first

meet them. Then later you find out that
they are evil villains who plan to take

over the world.

I bet he was lying about the dungeon.

How to Spell Read

Before school started, my mother told me that second grade was the most interesting grade because this was the year that I would be able to read chapter books all by myself. I already knew how to read, even though I had tried very hard not to learn.

You see, my friend Billy told me that you really don't have to know how to read. Billy says that when you grow up and make lots of money, you can pay people to read for you. That sounded good to me.

"I hate reading," I announced when Miss Daisy passed out some spelling worksheets.

"Me too!" agreed Miss Daisy.

"You do?" we all asked.

"Yup," she said. "I can't read a word."

"You can't?"

"Nope."

"You can't even spell the word *read*?" Michael Robinson asked.

"I don't have a clue," she said, scratching her head the same way she did when she told us she didn't know how to multiply four times four.

"Just sound it out, Miss Daisy!" Andrea suggested.

"*R-e-e-d?*" Miss Daisy said.

"No!" we all shouted.

"I give up," she said. "Do any of you know how to spell the word *read*?"

"*R-e-a-d*," we all chanted.

"Wow! I didn't know that!" marveled Miss Daisy. "You have taught me a lot today."

"How did you get to teach second grade if you don't even know how to spell *read*?" asked Ryan.

"Well, I figured that second graders don't know how to spell very well, so it wouldn't matter whether or not I could spell."

"I know how to spell lots of hard words," Andrea Young announced.

"Me too," everybody else said.

"Really?" Miss Daisy said. "Like what?"

Everybody started shouting out words and how to spell them, but Miss Daisy stopped us and made us take turns. She had each of us go up to the chalkboard and write three words we knew.

I wrote *tonight*, *writing* and *McDonald's*.

By the time we were done, the whole chalkboard was filled with words. There wasn't even any room left for more.

"Wow!" Miss Daisy said. "You kids have taught me so much this morning. I'm really glad I decided to become a teacher."

Miss Daisy Is Crazy!

In the lunchroom I opened my lunchbox and saw that my mom had packed me a peanut butter and jelly sandwich. I traded it with Michael Robinson for his potato chips. Everybody was talking about Miss Daisy.

"Miss Daisy is crazy," Ryan said.

"She's the weirdest teacher I ever had," said Emily. "She can't read, she can't write, and she can't even do arithmetic.

What kind of a teacher is that?"

"A bad one," I said.

"Hey, I just thought of something," Michael Robinson was able to say even though his mouth was filled with peanut

butter. "Do you think that maybe Miss Daisy isn't really a teacher at all?"

"What do you mean?" Ryan asked.

"Maybe she's an impostor," said Andrea.

"An impostor? What's that?" I asked. "Somebody who imposts?"

"No, silly. An impostor is somebody who pretends to be somebody else," Andrea explained. "She might be a fake teacher."

"Maybe Miss Daisy is really a jewel thief or a bank robber," I guessed. "Maybe she snuck into the school and is hiding so the police won't catch her."

"I think *you're* the one who's crazy." Andrea giggled, choking on her milk.

But what if Miss Daisy *was* a bank robber? Or she could be a horse thief or a cattle rustler or somebody who parks where there is a yellow line on the curb. My head was starting to fill with all kinds of awful things Miss Daisy could be.

"Maybe Miss Daisy kidnapped our real teacher and is holding her for ransom!" I suggested.

"Wow, you think so?" Emily asked, looking all scared.

"What's ransom?" asked Ryan.

"My mom tells me I'm handsome," Michael Robinson claimed.

"Not *handsome*! *Ransom*!" said Andrea. "I don't know what it is, but whenever somebody is kidnapped, they get held for it."

"In cartoons people who get kidnapped are always tied up to railroad tracks," I reminded everybody. "Maybe our real teacher is tied up to some railroad tracks right now!"

"We've got to save her!" said Emily, and she went running out of the lunchroom.

"Wait a minute," said Michael Robinson. "That doesn't make sense. If Miss Daisy can't even read or do arithmetic, how is

she going to be able to kidnap a teacher and tie her to railroad tracks?"

"She doesn't look like a kidnapper to me," Ryan said.

"We should tell Principal Klutz," said Andrea. "He'll know what to do."

"No!" I shouted. "Don't you see how good we have it? If we tell Principal Klutz how dumb Miss Daisy is, he will fire her and replace her with a real teacher. A real teacher who knows reading and writing and arithmetic. We'll have to learn all that stuff. You don't want that, do you?"

"No way!" said Michael Robinson.

"I don't care if she is an impostor or a bank robber or a kidnapper," I said. "I like her. I say we keep her."

"Me too," Michael Robinson agreed. "I think she's cool."

"Okay, let's not tell anybody," I said. "It will be our little secret."

We all agreed. Our lips would be sealed. But not sealed with glue or anything. That would be gross.

The Most Genius Idea!

After lunch we had recess, which means we get to go out in the playground and run around. Miss Daisy said we needed to burn off energy.

"Now this is more my style," I announced when we got outside. I made a beeline for the monkey bars. Then

me and some other kids hit the swings. After that all the boys had a contest to see who could spin around in circles the longest without throwing up. Michael Robinson won. Then we all sat down on the grass.

Even though Miss Daisy was pretty cool, we all agreed that we hated school. We made a promise to one another that we would hate school forever, even if we changed our minds and decided that we liked school.

That's when Ryan came up with the most genius idea in the history of the world.

This was his idea: We should buy the school.

Ryan told us that his father worked for this big company and that once his father's company bought some other company just like you would go into a store and buy a candy bar. Ryan said it happens all the time. He said he didn't see any reason why we couldn't buy the school just like that.

"If we bought the school, what would we do with it?" Michael Robinson asked.

"We could do anything we want with it. We'd own it."

"Could we turn it into a video-game

arcade?" I asked.

"Sure, why not? Instead of teaching reading and writing and arithmetic, we could teach kids how to play video games."

"And we could ride skateboards in the hallways?" asked Michael Robinson.

"Sure we could," Ryan said, "if we owned it."

I got all excited, because if there's one thing that I like to do almost as much as playing football, it's playing video games.

Oh, and riding skateboards. I started emptying out my pockets. I had a nickel, three pennies, and a LifeSaver. The other boys emptied their pockets too. We separated all the pennies, nickels, and dimes into little piles. Then we added up all the money. We had one dollar and thirty-two cents.

"Wow!" Michael Robinson said. "That's a lot of money!"

"I don't think it's enough to buy a school," said Ryan, who knew a thing or two about financial matters because his father worked for this big company.

"Well, how much do you need to buy a school?" I asked.

"Beats me," said Ryan. "We'd better ask Miss Daisy."

We all rushed inside after recess and asked Miss Daisy how much it would cost to buy the school.

"Gee, I don't know," said Miss Daisy, who didn't seem to know much of anything. "Why do you want to buy the school?"

"We want to turn it into a video-game arcade," I told her.

"What a great idea!" She beamed. "I love video games. There are so many schools and so few video-game arcades. It makes perfect sense to turn some of those schools into video-game arcades. I'll arrange a meeting with Mr. Klutz tomorrow so we can ask him if we can buy the school. But right now, we have to go to Mrs. Cooney's office."

Mrs. Cooney's office is down the hall from our class. She says she's the school nurse, but personally I think she's a spy. I'll tell you why. There's this big poster on her wall that says this:

I tried to read it, and it didn't make any sense at all. Even Andrea Young didn't know how to read the poster, and she knows everything. I think Mrs. Cooney has created a secret code, and she's using the poster to send mystery spy messages. I will have to keep an eye on her.

When we walked into Mrs. Cooney's office, she had us all line up in size order. I was one of the shortest kids, so I had to stand in the front of the line. Then Mrs. Cooney told us to take off our shoes. At first I thought she didn't want us to track mud all over her office. But then she told us that she was going to weigh and measure us. Obviously she is trying to gather information about us, because that is what spies do.

My friend Billy says that the heavier you are, the smarter you are, because heavy people have bigger brains. But I think Billy just says that because he is overweight. I weighed fifty-two pounds.

Mrs. Cooney showed us this awesome ruler she has. It is made of metal and stretches out six feet long. When she presses a button, the whole thing shoots into her hand and disappears like magic. That is cool! I'll bet she has lots of other spy tools too.

She wouldn't let us play with her magic ruler, but Mrs. Cooney ran around measuring everything. She showed us that the bench we were sitting on was seventeen inches high. The door to her office was thirty inches across. And her foot was twelve inches long.

"Hey, my foot is a foot!" Mrs. Cooney exclaimed.

"Aren't all feet feet?" I asked.

"Some feet are less than a foot, and some feet are more than a foot," she replied. "But my foot is exactly a foot."

I had no idea what she was talking about.

Mrs. Cooney

wrapped the meas-
uring tape around
her forehead and
announced, "Look!
My head is almost
two feet in circumference!"

I knew that circumference was the distance all the way around a circle and
diameter was the distance through the
middle of a circle.

"What's the diameter of your head, Mrs.

Cooney?" I asked. Everybody laughed, even though I didn't say anything funny.

"That would be hard to measure. But isn't measuring things fun?" Mrs. Cooney asked. "I wonder how much the scale weighs."

Mrs. Cooney started to measure and weigh more things, but Miss Daisy said we had to go back to class.

What Do You Want to Be?

At the end of the day, Miss Daisy sat on the floor and we all sat around her. She told us to talk about what we want to be when we grow up.

"I want to be a veterinarian," said Andrea Young.

"Does anyone know what the word

veterinarian means?" asked Miss Daisy.

"That's somebody who doesn't eat meat," said Michael Robinson.

"It is not!" I said. "That's a vegetarian. A veterinarian is somebody who fought in a war."

"That's a veteran," Miss Daisy said. "Andrea, would you like to tell the class what a veterinarian does?"

"A veterinarian is an animal doctor."

That Andrea Young thinks she knows everything. But for once, I knew she was wrong.

"Animals can't be doctors," I said.

Everybody laughed, even though I didn't say anything funny. Miss Daisy said a veterinarian is a doctor who takes care of animals. That made a lot more sense than that dumb thing Andrea said.

Emily was next and she said she wanted to grow up and become a nurse in a hospital.

"Why do you want to do that?" I asked. "People come into hospitals all sick and injured, their arms falling off, their guts hanging out. . . ."

"A.J.!" Miss Daisy said in her serious voice.

Emily got all upset and ran out of the room crying.

"What did I say?" I asked.

"What do you want to be when you grow up, A.J.?" Miss Daisy asked.

"I'm going to be a famous football

player," I said.

"Really? And why did you choose that field?"

"Because I love football," I said, "and if I was a football player, I wouldn't have to read or write or do arithmetic or go to school. My friend Billy told me that foot-

ball players are really dumb."

"Your friend told you that?" said Miss Daisy.

"Yeah, Billy is really smart. He also told me that if you dig a hole deep enough, you can dig all the way to China. And if you fall into that hole, you'd fall all the way through the Earth and pop right out the other side. And you'd be moving so fast that you'd shoot all the way into outer space."

Michael Robinson said that sounded cool. He decided that instead of becoming a firefighter, he wanted to become one of those hole-digging astronauts.

Emily came back into the room with

a tissue. Everybody else went around in a circle saying what they wanted to be. This girl named Lindsay said she wanted to be a singer. Ryan said he wanted to be a businessman like his dad.

Andrea Young said that if she couldn't be a veterinarian, she wanted to be a teacher like Miss Daisy. Then she gave Miss Daisy a big smile.

I hate her.

Bonbons and Footballs

The next day, Miss Daisy brought in a box with ribbons on it and told us she had a surprise.

"What's in the box?" we pleaded.

"It's a secret."

"Pleeeeeeeeeeeeeeeeease?"

"Well, okay," she said, opening the box.

"It's bonbons!"

Miss Daisy said she thought we might be able to use them for arithmetic problems so we could learn together. She put the bonbons on the table in the front of the room. There must have been twenty or thirty of them. "Can somebody think up an arithmetic problem using bonbons?" she asked. "Andrea?"

"If you had three bonbons in a box," said Andrea as she put three bonbons into her pencil box, "and you had three boxes just like that, how many bonbons would you have all together?"

Miss Daisy looked at Andrea's pencil box for a long time, counting in her head and on her fingers. Any dummy would know that three boxes with three bonbons in each box would equal nine bonbons. Three times three is nine. But Miss Daisy didn't seem to know that. Finally she just opened up Andrea's pencil box and popped the three bonbons into her mouth.

"Who cares how many bonbons I would have?" she asked. "As long as I get to eat some of them!"

Miss Daisy really needs a lot of help with arithmetic.

After she had eaten her bonbons, Miss Daisy passed out bonbons for all of us and we had a bonbon party. Then she said that was enough arithmetic for the day and asked what we wanted to talk about for the rest of our math time. "Football!" I shouted.

Miss Daisy didn't like that I talked without raising my hand first. Personally, I don't see what raising my hand has to do with talking. I don't talk with my hands.

But she did let me talk, and I told her that football is just about my favoritest thing in the world and I know all about it. My dad takes me to every game of the Chargers, a professional football team.

"Maybe you can help me," Miss Daisy said. "I always wondered how long is a football field?"

"A hundred yards," I told her. "Anybody knows that."

"Wow! That's a big field. With a field that big, how can you and your father see what's going on?"

"My dad always tries to get us seats near the fifty-yard line," I said. "They're the best tickets."

"Why?" Miss Daisy asked.

"Because the fifty-yard line is right in the middle of the field."

"Does that mean that half of a hundred yards would be fifty yards?" she asked.

"Yup."

"I see," Miss Daisy said. "So if you know there are a hundred yards on a football field, do you know how many pennies there are in a dollar? Andrea?"

"A hundred!" hollered Andrea Young. "Just like a football field!"

"Really?" said Miss Daisy. "So if half the football field is fifty yards, how many pennies are in half a dollar?"

"Fifty!" Michael Robinson shouted.

"Because fifty is half of a hundred and fifty plus fifty makes a hundred!"

"And half of fifty must be twenty-five because two quarters is fifty cents!" added Emily.

"And four quarters makes a dollar!" Ryan exclaimed.

"And four quarters makes a football game, too!" Miss Daisy shouted, jumping

up and down with excitement.

"Wait a minute," I said. "I thought you told us we were finished with arithmetic."

"This wasn't arithmetic," she told us. "It was football."

"Well, okay," I said. "Just as long as you weren't trying to sneak arithmetic into our conversation about football."

"Would I do that?" Miss Daisy asked, and then she winked at me.

Sometimes it's hard to tell if Miss Daisy is serious or not.

A Lot
of Books!

On Thursday Principal Klutz came into our class. He was wearing a hat, which almost made him look like a regular person who had hair on his head.

"I have to go to a meeting," Principal Klutz told us, "but I heard that some of you second graders had something important you wanted to discuss with me."

Miss Daisy said that I could ask my question.

"Can we buy the school?"

"Hmmm," Principal Klutz said. "Hmmm" is what grown-ups say instead of "er" or "um" or "uh" when they don't know what to say.

"Why do you want to buy the school?" Principal Klutz asked.

"Because we want to turn it into a video-game arcade," I told him.

"I see," the principal said. "Schools cost a lot of money."

"How much?" I asked. "If you tell us how much it will cost, we'll raise the money."

"I'll tell you what," Principal Klutz said. "I can't sell you the school, but I can rent

it to you for a night. Do you know the difference between buying and renting?"

Andrea Young got her hand up first, as
usual.

"When you buy a video, you get to
keep it forever," she said. "If you rent it,
you have to return it to the video store in
a couple of days."

"That's right," the principal said. "Would you be interested in renting the school for a night?"

"How much would that cost?" I asked.

"One million pages," Principal Klutz replied.

"Huh?"

"If you kids read a million pages in books, you can turn the school into a video-game arcade for one night."

A million pages! That sounded like a lot of books.

"How about a thousand pages?" I suggested.

"A million," said Principal Klutz. "That's my final offer. Take it or leave it."

"Would it be okay if some of the other

classes helped us out?" Miss Daisy asked.

"Certainly," Principal Klutz said. "The more the merrier. And I'll tell you what I'm going to do. If the kids in this school read a million pages, I will come to the big video-game night dressed in a gorilla suit."

"You've got a deal!" I said, rushing forward to shake Principal Klutz's hand.

In my head I was already hatching a plan.

Put Those Books Away

As soon as I got home from school, I went up to my big sister Amy's room.

Amy is in fifth grade, so she knows lots of things.

"You've got to help me!" I said. "If the school reads a million pages in books, Principal Klutz will put on a gorilla suit and let us turn the school into a video-game arcade!"

"I would do anything to see that," Amy said.

Amy knows how to work the computer really well. She helped me make posters that said LET'S TURN OUR SCHOOL INTO A VIDEO-GAME ARCADE! and LET'S TURN PRINCIPAL KLUTZ INTO A GORILLA!

We tacked the posters up all over Main Street. Amy sent e-mails and instant messages to all the kids in the fifth grade. The next morning we tacked the posters up all over school. I passed them out to the kids I saw. Mrs. Roopy, the school librarian, said we could put up some posters in the library. Miss Lazar, the custodian, said we could put some up in the lunchroom and the bathrooms. Mr. Loring, the music teacher, said we could put some up in the music room.

By the middle of the day, everyone in the school was reading like crazy! Kids were reading during lunch. Kids were reading during recess! Kids were plowing their way through books and then running to the school library to ask Mrs. Roopy if they could check out more. I read a book about frogs, and I don't even care anything about frogs.

Some of the teachers were starting to get mad, because kids were reading books when they were supposed to be doing other things.

"Please put those books away," Miss Daisy had to tell us. "It's time for reading."

Miss Daisy said she was sorry that she wouldn't be able to help us very much because she didn't know how to read. But she was nice enough to draw a big mural in the hallway with a giant thermometer on it. Every time we read a lot of pages, she would make the temperature line on the thermometer go up. At the top of the thermometer were the words *One million*.

Soon kids were bursting into our room and yelling, "Mrs. Biggs's class has read another five hundred pages!" and "Miss

Hasenfratz says to add another six hundred pages!" It was fun watching the temperature go up.

At the end of a week, our school had read almost a half a million pages!

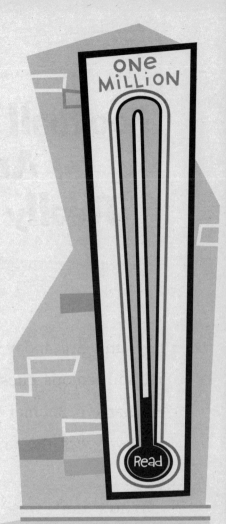

10

Football Players Are Really Dumb

"Boys and girls, today we have a very special and famous guest," Miss Daisy said. "His name is Boomer Wiggins."

"Wow!" was the first thing everybody said.

"Who's he?" was the second thing everybody said.

But I knew who Boomer Wiggins was. Because Boomer Wiggins was my hero. He was the quarterback of my favorite football team, the Chargers! Wow! A real football player right in our classroom! Miss Daisy told us that Boomer Wiggins had a daughter in fourth grade, and that's why he was spending the day at our school.

When Boomer Wiggins walked into the class, everybody gasped. He was really big and had so many muscles that they poked right against his shirt! We all crowded around him, and Boomer let us feel his arm muscles. I couldn't even get my hands around them! Then Boomer picked up Emily with one hand!

He was amazing. Then
he gave each of us
a little plastic
football, and he
signed his name
on each one.

"Does
anybody
have any
questions?"
Boomer asked.

"Do you like
knocking guys
on their butts?"
I asked.

Everybody
laughed,

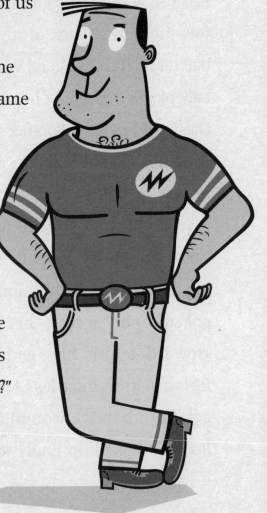

even though I didn't say anything that was funny. Miss Daisy said it was "butt," not "butts," because a person only has one butt. But I said a butt was divided into two halves, so really it could be "butts." Miss Daisy said that was enough of that talk. I said she shouldn't be complaining because she was the one who started it.

"I don't like knocking people down," Boomer told us, "but sometimes we have to because it's part of the game."

"Mr. Wiggins," asked Miss Daisy, "is it true that football players are really dumb?"

We all gasped. I was afraid Boomer Wiggins might knock Miss Daisy on her butt.

"Excuse me?" Boomer said, like he wasn't sure if he had heard the question.

"Well, somebody once told me that if you play football, you don't have to know how to read or write or do arithmetic or go to school."

"Who told you that?" Boomer asked Miss Daisy.

Everybody looked at me. I slid down so that my head was almost under my desk, and I hid behind my notebook.

"Oh, a good friend of mine told me," Miss Daisy said. "Is it true?"

"If I didn't go to school, I never could have become a football player," Boomer told us. "I have to read and study my playbook very carefully. I have to write letters to my fans. Every week I have to study very hard to get ready for the next game."

"Did you go to college?" asked Miss Daisy.

"Yes," Boomer said, "and when my football career is over, I plan to go back to school so I can become a doctor."

"Wow!" I said. "I want to go to college someday so I can become a doctor and knock guys on their butts. I mean butt."

Everybody laughed, even though I didn't say anything funny. Then, to prove how smart he was, Boomer Wiggins read us a book and passed out bookmarks that said "Achieve Your Goal by Reading" on them.

Miss Daisy said that even though Boomer read the book to us, we could still add fifty-two pages to the total number of pages we've read.

The temperature level on the thermometer in the hallway kept getting higher and higher.

We Rule the School!

Finally the big moment arrived. It was Andrea Young (of course!) who read the one-millionth page. We all cheered when Miss Daisy went out in the hallway and filled in the top of the thermometer all the way up to the words *One million.*

That Friday night, everybody in the

whole school showed up at school. Can you believe it? I actually couldn't wait to get to school . . . on the weekend! When we got there, a big banner was hanging over the front door that said WE READ A MILLION PAGES! on it. Principal Klutz was waiting for us. He was wearing a gorilla suit, just like he promised. Inside there

was a table of snacks and treats and juice.
Miss Daisy had brought in bonbons.

But best of all, the gym was filled wall
to wall with video games!

We Read A Million Pages!

I had never seen so many video games in my life. Families had brought in lots of TV sets, game systems, and games, and lined them up all around the gym. We could play all we wanted, and the only rule was that you had to take turns.

For the kids who didn't like video games, there were tables of board games set up in the middle of the gym. (I think they're called board games because you get so bored playing them.)

I played just about every video game in the gym. After a few hours of staring into screens, I had a splitting headache, my hands hurt, and I thought my eyes were going to fall out of my head.

It was the greatest night of my life.

Poor
Miss Daisy

Monday at school, we had social studies. Miss Daisy said she was really sorry, but she didn't know anything at all about social studies and that we would have to help her.

"I don't even know the name of the first president of the United States," she told us.

"You don't?" we all said.

"I haven't a clue."

"It was George Washington!" we all shouted.

"Really?" Miss Daisy said with a wink. "Never heard of him."

I was beginning to suspect that Miss Daisy might have been just pretending that she didn't know anything all along. One day I caught her looking at a piece of paper, and her eyes were moving back and forth like she was watching a Ping-Pong game.

"Hey, you're reading!" I said.

"I am not!" she insisted. "You know I can't read."

"Then how come your eyes are moving

back and forth like you're watching a Ping-Pong game?"

"I—I was just thinking about this great Ping-Pong game I saw once," she replied. "It was great. You should have been there."

Maybe she was joking, and maybe she wasn't. You can never tell with Crazy Miss Daisy.

If it turns out that Miss Daisy really doesn't know anything, I feel a little sorry for her. The kids in our school had read a million pages, and she couldn't read one page. The kids in our class knew how to spell, and do arithmetic and social studies. She hardly knew anything at all!

"Don't feel bad, Miss Daisy," I told her. "We'll teach you reading, writing, and arithmetic. And we won't tell Principal Klutz how dumb you are." She gave me a big hug.

It will be hard work teaching Miss Daisy everything that she doesn't know. I think that by the end of the year, if the whole class works together, we just might bring her up to second-grade level.

But it won't be easy.

Mr. Klutz Is Nuts!

Dan Gutman

Pictures by Jim Paillot

HarperTrophy®
An Imprint of HarperCollinsPublishers

To Emma

The Flying Principal

"Watch out!" somebody screamed.

Mr. Klutz, the principal of my school, was tearing down the sidewalk on a skateboard! It was early morning, just before the school bell was about to ring.

Mr. Klutz must have built up too much speed coming down the hill. He was

1

weaving in and around the kids and their parents, totally out of control. Most principals are really serious and dignified. They look like they were *born* as grown-ups! But not Mr. Klutz. He's more like a grown-up kid. When he isn't skateboarding to school, he rides his motorcycle, his scooter, or wears his in-line skates.

"Runaway principal!" some kid shouted. "Run for your lives!"

The skateboard must have hit a crack in the sidewalk, because the next thing

anybody knew, Mr. Klutz was flying through the air like a superhero. Kids and their parents were diving out of his way. Dogs were running in all directions.

Mr. Klutz crash-landed in the bushes at the front of the school. Luckily he was wearing a helmet, and he had knee pads and elbow pads on over his clothes. Everybody stopped for a second, because Mr. Klutz was just lying there in the

bushes without moving. We weren't sure if he was alive.

"Good morning, Mr. Klutz," said Mrs. Cooney, the school nurse, as she walked past.

"Good morning, Mrs. Cooney," he replied.

"Beautiful day, isn't it?"

"Lovely."

Then Mr. Klutz got up, brushed himself off, and walked up the front steps, like it was totally normal for a principal to skateboard to school and crash headfirst into the bushes.

Mr. Klutz is nuts!

Big Trouble

"That's the last straw, A.J.," my teacher, Miss Daisy, told me. "I want you to go to the principal's office!"

"I didn't do anything!" I protested.

My name is A.J. and I hate school. Why do we have to learn so much stuff? If you ask me, by the time you get to second grade you already know enough stuff to last you a lifetime. School is way overrated.

My mom says that all eight-year-old boys have to go to school, so I guess there's nothing I can do about it. But when I grow up, I'm going to be a professional hockey player. You don't have to

know how to read or write or do math to shoot a puck into a net.

Actually, that's what I was doing when my teacher, Miss Daisy, sent me to the principal's office.

You see, me and my friends Michael and Ryan were playing hockey with a tennis ball during recess. We were shooting the ball at a tree to score a goal. I shot one wild, and it landed over by a bunch of girls in our class.

"Ouch! That hit me!" shouted this girl named Annette. She was rubbing her leg like she had been hit by a train or something. It was just a tennis ball! Annette is such a crybaby.

"Hey, A.J.!" Michael hollered. "That counts as a goal!"

"How come?" I asked. "I missed the tree."

"Well, you did hit the puck into Annette. Get it? Annette? A net? Annette?" Well, after me and Ryan got it, we thought that was just about the funniest joke in the history of the world.

Miss Daisy didn't think it was very funny, though. She was already mad at me because I had forgotten to bring in a current-event article for the third week in a row.

That's when she said it was the last straw and I had to go to Mr. Klutz's office.

The Principal Is Your Pal

The principal is like the king of the school. He gets to tell everybody what to do and where to go. That is cool! If I can't be a professional hockey player when I grow up, I want to be a principal so I can boss teachers around.

My friend Billy from around the

corner, who was in second grade last year, told me that principals have a dungeon down in the basement of the school where they torture kids who misbehave. I don't know if Billy's telling the truth or not. But one time we had gym class and we passed by this open door in the basement and there were all kinds of scary-looking things in there. Michael said he saw chains hanging from the ceiling over a chair with straps on the arms and legs, so I guess that's what Mr. Klutz uses to torture bad kids.

I was scared. I had never been to the principal's office before. On the way there, I stopped into the boy's bathroom. Maybe I could dig a tunnel out of the school and escape, I thought. My friend Billy told me he saw that in a war movie once. These guys dug their way out of prison camp with a spoon. But I didn't have a spoon. And I didn't want to touch the floor of the bathroom anyway. Yuck!

When I got to Mr. Klutz's office, his secretary made me sit in a chair for about a million hours. Mr. Klutz's door was closed the whole time. I wondered if he was torturing some other kid. I didn't hear any screams or anything.

Finally the secretary said I could go inside. I opened the door and was surprised to see Mr. Klutz was hanging upside down from a bar near the ceiling. He had on boots that were attached to the bar.

"What are you doing up there?" I asked.

"Oh, just hanging around," Mr. Klutz said as he pulled himself out of his boots and jumped down onto the floor. "When the blood rushes to my head, it helps me think."

Well, I know that blood rushing to your head doesn't help you grow hair, because Mr. Klutz had no hair on his

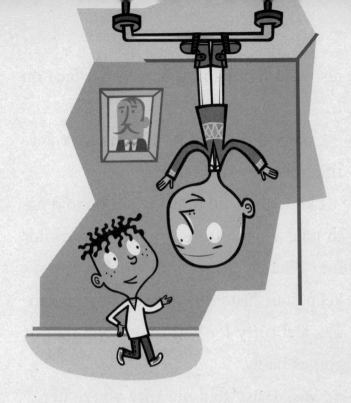

head at all. He was bald as a balloon. Mr. Klutz's office looked pretty much like my dad's office, except he had a big snowboarding poster on the wall and a foosball table in the corner. Oh, and he also had a punching bag with a face on it.

Come to think of it, it didn't look anything like my dad's office.

I kept my head down when he told me to take a seat, so he would feel sorry for me. When you get into trouble, always keep your head down, because if grown-ups feel sorry for you they won't punish you as badly.

"Miss Daisy told me why you're here," Mr. Klutz said, "but I'd like to hear your side of the story."

"Miss Daisy thinks I stole some straws," I told him.

"What makes you think that, A.J.?"

"Well, she was all mad at me and she said, 'That's the last straw!' Then she told me to go to your office. I swear I didn't take any straws. I don't even know where she keeps the straws."

"I see," Mr. Klutz said, rubbing his chin. "I thought it had something to do with a hockey game that got out of control. And there's this little matter of forgetting to bring in current events."

"Well, that too."

Mr. Klutz didn't look like he was going to torture me. In fact, he didn't look mad at all.

"You may not believe this," he told me, "but I was a boy once."

"Just once?" I asked. "I'm a boy *all* the time."

"No, what I mean is, I used to be young like you."

"I'll bet you were really good in school," I said.

"No, actually, it was just the opposite," the principal told me. "I didn't like school at all, and I wasn't a very good student."

"Really?" I figured that anybody who grew up to be a principal must have loved school as a kid. Why else would you want to hang around a school all day as a grown-up? Except maybe to boss teachers around.

"When I was a boy, I could never sit

still," Mr. Klutz said. "I wanted to run around all the time. I didn't have the motivation to do my schoolwork. Do you know what motivation is, A.J.?"

"It's like a motor inside you that makes you want to do stuff," I said. "That's why it's called motor-vation."

"I guess you could say that," Mr. Klutz said. "Sometimes my mother would give me a little reward if I did a good job on my homework. A piece of candy, for instance. You see, while I didn't like school, I certainly did like candy. So I would try hard in school in order to get the candy. Does that make sense to you?"

"Well, sure."

"A.J., if I were to give you some candy, do you think it might help you remember to bring in your current event next time?"

"My parents told me never to take candy from strangers," I told him.

"I'm not a stranger," Mr. Klutz said. "Did you ever hear anyone say 'your principal is your pal'? If you need to spell the word *principal*, you can always remember, your princi*pal* is your *p-a-l*. Get it?"

"Well, if you put it that way, I suppose I could take some candy."

Mr. Klutz reached into his desk drawer and pulled out a chocolate bar. It was the kind with marshmallow inside, and caramel. My mouth was watering. "Go easy with the hockey. And let's see if you can remember to bring in that current event tomorrow," he said as he handed me the candy bar. "Don't tell anyone about this, okay? It's

just a little secret between you and me."

"Okay!"

I ran out of the office just in case he had only given me the candy bar so he could tie me to a chair and torture me.

The Present

When I got back to the class, everybody looked at me. I guess they wanted to see if I was crying or bleeding or anything.

"Did Klutz bring you down into his torture chamber?" Ryan whispered when I sat in my seat.

"Nope," I said. "He gave me a present."

"What did he give you?"

"I can't tell you."

"Oh, come on!"

"I promised I wouldn't tell."

"I'll be your best friend."

"Well, okay. I'll show you at lunch."

During lunch, I sat at a table with my new best friend Ryan, Michael, smarty-pants Andrea, and Emily, who cries all the time even if she isn't hurt or anything. You should have seen their eyes bug out when I showed them the candy bar.

"Where did you get *that*?" Michael asked. "Your mom usually gives you carrot sticks for dessert."

"Mr. Klutz gave it to me," I explained.

"He's got a whole drawer filled with them."

"Why did he give you a candy bar?" asked Emily. I could tell she was jealous.

"Because I didn't bring in my current event," I explained.

"Wait a minute!" Andrea said, all angry and all. "You got sent to the principal's office for being bad, and instead of punishing you, he gave you a candy bar? That's not fair! I brought in *three* current events and I didn't get a candy bar."

"Maybe you should try not being so perfect all the time," I said. "You can have my carrot sticks, Andrea."

I love getting Andrea mad. She thinks

she knows everything. Whenever we have a homework assignment, she does extra work just to show Miss Daisy how smart she is and to make the rest of us look bad.

"Mr. Klutz told me he's my pal," I said, biting off a big piece of the chocolate bar right in front of Andrea's face. "He said I could come in for a candy bar any time I want one."

That last part wasn't exactly true, but it was fun to say anyway.

"The principal should give candy to students who complete their assignments," Andrea said. "Not to kids who don't."

"Yeah," Emily sniffed. She looked like

she might run out of the room crying like she usually does for no reason.

"I want to go to the principal's office!" my best friend Ryan announced.

"Me too!" Michael agreed. "I want a candy bar!"

They all watched while I finished off the candy. I licked the extra chocolate off my fingers and rubbed my tummy, just to make sure they would know how good it was.

My Big Mouth

It just so happens that I know of the perfect way to get sent to the principal's office. All you have to do is put a tack on the teacher's chair. My friend Billy told me he did this once and he got sent to the principal's office.

I waited until recess, when Andrea and

Emily ran off to play with the girls. Then I told the plan to my best friend Ryan and Michael.

"That's genius!" exclaimed my best friend Ryan.

"What if Miss Daisy gets hurt?" asked Michael.

"She won't get hurt," I told him. "She'll jump up so fast that she won't hardly feel it."

So at the end of recess, the three of us snuck back into our classroom. It was empty. Miss Daisy was eating in the teacher's room. Ryan pulled a tack out of the bulletin board and put it on Miss Daisy's chair. Then we ran out to the playground just as the end-of-recess bell was ringing. When we filed back into the class, Ryan, Michael, and I could barely look at one another because we were afraid we'd burst out laughing. I could hardly wait to see the look on Miss Daisy's face when she sat on her chair.

Well, when Miss Daisy sat down, the most amazing thing happened.

Nothing! She didn't jump up or any- thing. She just sat there. Me and Ryan and Michael looked at one another. How could she not feel that?

"She must have buns of steel!" Ryan whispered.

"She's like Superman."

Then I realized that I had forgotten to tell Ryan something very important. When you put a tack on the teacher's chair, you're supposed to put the tack a little bit on one side. When you put it in the middle of the chair, the tack sort of . . . well . . . you know, it doesn't have any target to hit, if you know what I mean.

Miss Daisy got up to do math, not even realizing there was a tack in her butt. When she turned around to write on the chalkboard, we could see the tack was just stuck there, hanging in the middle of her backside.

Me and Ryan and Michael thought we were going to die trying to keep ourselves from laughing. It was probably the funniest thing that had ever happened in the history of the world. You should have been there!

"Excuse me," said Andrea, raising her hand to ruin everybody's fun like always. "Miss Daisy, I think there's something stuck to your skirt."

Miss Daisy turned around and pulled out the tack. "Who did this?" she demanded.

"I did!" Ryan bragged.

"Go to the principal's office, Ryan."

"All right!" Ryan whispered, pumping his fist. "I'll be back in a few minutes with a candy bar!"

"Is there anyone else who wants to go to the principal's office?" Miss Daisy asked.

"I do!" said Michael.

"Can I go again?" I said.

"Hey, I asked first!" Michael complained.

"Quiet, both of you."

Miss Daisy pretended nothing unusual had happened and went back to her lesson, but I saw her look at her chair carefully before she sat down again.

A few minutes later Ryan came back to the classroom. Mr. Klutz was with him.

"So did he give you a candy bar?" I

whispered excitedly when Ryan sat down.

"No," Ryan whispered back. "When I told him that I thought he would give me a candy bar like he gave one to you, he got really upset. He told me he was going to call my parents and have them come in to talk about what happened. I think we're all in big trouble."

Oh, man! I decided that maybe it wouldn't be such a good idea to be best friends with Ryan anymore. I should have kept my big mouth shut about the candy bar.

6

The Chocolate Party

When I thought about it, putting a tack on Miss Daisy's chair was a pretty dumb thing to do.

Mr. Klutz went to the front of the class. I was sure he was going to bring all of us to the torture chamber in the basement. But he didn't look all that mad, considering what we had done.

"It has come to my attention that some of the students at our school need a little extra incentive to behave and work their hardest," Mr. Klutz said. "Do you know what the word *incentive* means?"

"An incentive is a reward that encourages a person to work harder to achieve something," Andrea announced, all proud of herself. She thinks she knows everything. I hate her.

"Very good, Andrea," said Mr. Klutz. "What sort of incentive might bring out the best work in the students of our school?"

"You could give us each a million dollars," suggested Michael.

"You could make summer vacation last all year long," I said.

"How about getting rid of homework?" asked Ryan.

Miss Daisy went to the front of the

room. "Mr. Klutz can't do those things," she said. "But remember when all the students in our school read a million pages in books, and as a reward we turned the gym into a video-game arcade? That was quite successful. Mr. Klutz even dressed up in a gorilla suit for the evening, if I recall."

"How about a chocolate party?" suggested Andrea.

"Yeah!" everybody yelled.

"Mmmm," said Miss Daisy. "I like that idea!"

We all got very excited, because if there is one thing that just about everybody loves, it's chocolate. Kids started shouting out things we could have at the party, like chocolate cupcakes and chocolate fudge and chocolate bunnies and chocolate ice cream and on and on and on.

"But wait a minute," Mr. Klutz said. "What are you going to do to earn this chocolate party?"

"We could read another million pages," suggested Ryan.

"We did that already," Emily said.

"How about a million math problems?" I said.

"What a wonderful idea!" Miss Daisy beamed. Ever since we taught her how to add and subtract, Miss Daisy loved math.

"Math is hard," Ryan said. "How about a hundred math problems?"

"One million math problems," Mr. Klutz insisted. "That's my final offer. Take it or leave it."

"We'll take it!" we all yelled.

"Agreed. If the kids in our school do one million math problems, I'll throw a party with so much chocolate, you'll be sick for a week."

"I'll bring the bonbons," Miss Daisy volunteered.

"Hooray!" we all yelled, except for Ryan who looked all mad.

"I'm not going to spend my free time doing math," Ryan said. "I hate math. I wouldn't do extra math if you kissed a pig on the lips."

"Okay, as an added incentive," Mr.

Klutz said, "on the night of the party, I will kiss a pig on the lips. Have a nice day."

"All right!"

What a cool, wacky guy Mr. Klutz is! He is the coolest principal in the history of the world.

Teacher for a Day

The news about the big chocolate party blew through the school like a hurricane. Even kids who were allergic to chocolate wanted to go, just so they could see Mr. Klutz kiss a pig on the lips.

"Where is he going to get a pig?" Ryan asked during lunch the next day.

"He could try A.J.'s house," Andrea said.

"That's so funny I forgot to laugh," I said.

"I'm not entirely sure that pigs have lips," said Emily.

"Of course they have lips," I insisted. "If they didn't have lips, how could they whistle?"

"You know," Ryan pointed out, "Mr. Klutz is just trying to trick us into doing lots of math problems. That's why we're having a chocolate party."

"Who cares?" Michael said. "As long as we get the chocolate."

"I think that only students who do math problems should be allowed to come to the chocolate party," said Andrea.

"Could you possibly be any more boring?" I asked her.

As it turned out, everybody was doing math problems. The whole school started doing math problems like crazy. Even Ryan. You would have thought that Mr. Klutz was giving us gold and diamonds instead of chocolate.

"I did math problems for twenty minutes last night," Ryan bragged while we were waiting for Miss Daisy after recess.

"Oh, yeah?" Michael said. "Well, I did math problems for forty minutes last night.

Forty is twice as many as twenty. See? I just did another math problem right there!"

"Well I did math problems for an hour last night," I said. "That's fifty whole minutes."

"An hour is sixty minutes, dumbhead," Andrea told me.

I was going to tell her that *Sixty Minutes* was a TV show my parents watch, but Mr. Klutz suddenly burst into our classroom. He told us that Miss Daisy had a dentist appointment and we would have a substitute teacher for the rest of the afternoon . . . Mr. Klutz!

We all gasped.

"You're not a teacher!" I told him.

"I used to be a teacher," he said. "I taught for many years before I became a principal."

"What did you teach?" Ryan asked.

"Physics," he said.

"What's that?" I asked.

"Is that like phys ed?" asked Michael.

"Mr. Klutz, do you know that this is second grade?" Andrea pointed out. "Physics is something high school students study."

"Poppycock!" said Mr. Klutz. "You're never too young to learn something new. You may find you're smarter than you think."

"Well, if you say so."

"Physics is the study of motion and energy and force," he said. "For example, if I take a blackboard eraser in one hand and a book in the other hand, and I drop them at the same time, which one will hit the floor first?"

"The eraser!" I said. "It's smaller and lighter, so it will fall faster. Just like small, light kids run faster than big, heavy kids."

"No, the book will hit the floor first!" insisted Ryan. "Bigger and heavier things build up more speed than little things."

"I think they'll both hit the floor at the same time," said Andrea.

"Let's do a test," said Mr. Klutz.

He put the eraser in his left hand and a

paperback book in his right hand. Then he climbed on top of Miss Daisy's desk and held both objects up in the air. Then he dropped them.

The eraser and the book hit the ground at the exact same moment.

"I told you so," said Andrea. I think I hate her more every day.

"According to the laws of physics, all objects fall at the exact same rate," Mr. Klutz told us. "See? You're learning physics in second grade!"

"Wait a minute!" said Michael. "That's not a fair test because the eraser and the book are almost the same size and weight."

"Yeah," Ryan said. "Try it with different objects."

"Okay," Mr. Klutz said as he picked up a pencil off Miss Daisy's desk. Then he went over to the windowsill, where Miss

Daisy kept her collection of stuffed animals. He picked up a giraffe that was almost as big as I am. "Would this be a fair test?" he asked.

"Yeah!" we all shouted.

"Now, which object do you think will hit the floor first?" he said as he climbed up on top of Miss Daisy's desk again.

"The pencil!" some of us shouted.

"The giraffe!" other kids yelled.

"I think they will both hit the floor at the same instant," said Andrea.

"Okay, let's do a test," said Mr. Klutz.

As he raised both his arms in the air, Mr. Klutz put his foot on a crayon that was sitting on Miss Daisy's desk. It rolled a little. His foot slipped. He wobbled for a moment, trying to keep his balance. Then he pitched headfirst off the desk.

"Watch out!"

Crash!

When he hit the floor, the pencil and the giraffe went flying, and Mr. Klutz's arms and legs went in different directions. It was just about the funniest thing that ever happened in the history of the world. You should have been there.

We all ran over to see if Mr. Klutz was okay. He was holding his leg and moaning.

"See?" Andrea said. "All *three* objects hit the ground at the same time. The pencil, the giraffe, and Mr. Klutz. So I was right."

I hate her.

Mr. Klutz
Puckers Up

When Mr. Klutz got back from the hospital, we were all relieved to hear that he hadn't broken any bones. He was limping, though, and told us he would have to use a cane for a week.

We were afraid he might call off the chocolate party, but he was more excited about it than ever.

Everybody in the whole school got involved doing math problems so we could win the party, even the teachers.

During library period, Mrs. Roopy asked us questions like, "If the library had a hundred books and you checked out fifty of them, how many would be left in the library?"

During music period, Ms. Hynde asked us questions like, "If the school only has ten trumpets and six kids sign up to take trumpet lessons, how many more kids can sign up for trumpet lessons?"

Miss Daisy made a big tote board so we would know how many math problems we had completed. Every day, she tallied up all the math problems on her tote board.

It wasn't long before the school had finished a million math problems.

Andrea did the problem that put us

over the top—of course. I hate her.

On the night of the chocolate party, you should have seen the gym! They had music and games, and tables were set up with chocolate chip cookies, chocolate cake, chocolate muffins, and even broccoli covered with chocolate. Yuck!

By the end of the party, I thought I was going to throw up. It was the greatest night of my life.

At nine o'clock somebody came in with this big pig on a leash. I don't know where they got it. The zoo, I guess. We all watched as the pig was brought over to Mr. Klutz. He wrinkled his face up and acted like he was all disgusted

(Mr. Klutz, that is, not the pig).

When he bent over and kissed the pig
on the lips, the whole school went crazy.

Even the pig freaked out, oinking and squealing and running around the gym until the grown-ups were able to catch it.

It was a real Kodak moment, if you ask me.

9

I Pledge Allegiance to Mr. Klutz

"I want to congratulate all you kids," Mr. Klutz said over the loudspeaker on Monday morning during announcements. "You did it! One million math problems. That's quite an accomplishment! See, all you needed was a little incentive.

"This has been such a huge success that

I have decided to challenge you again," he continued. "Election Day is coming up in November. This is a very important day in America. I think every child in this school should write an essay about what it means to have elections. And if you achieve this goal by Election Day, I will climb the flagpole in front of the school and recite the Pledge of Allegience when I get to the top."

"I hope he doesn't hurt himself again," said Emily.

"I'll write my essay during recess," said Andrea, who always does everything the second any grown-up tells her to instead of waiting as long as possible, like a normal kid.

"Couldn't we just write one essay for the whole class?" I asked Miss Daisy. "That would be a lot easier."

Mr. Klutz's voice came out of the loud-speaker again. "I know some of you will ask if you can write a class essay. The answer is no. If you want to see me shinny up the flagpole, each student must write their own essay. That's my final offer. Take it or leave it. And I'll tell you what. When we have all the essays, I will send them to the president to read. Have a nice day."

The thought of the president of the United States reading our personal words was pretty cool, I had to admit. Everybody finished their Election Day essays so quickly, we were done a week before Election Day. Some kids (like Andrea) even wrote two essays.

On the morning of Election Day, all the students and teachers gathered on the grass in front of the school. Mr. Klutz came out of the door. He was wearing a red, white, and blue Uncle Sam costume. He also had on sneakers and one of those harnesses that lumberjacks use to climb trees. His leg was all better and he didn't walk with a cane anymore.

We all let out a roar when Mr. Klutz started to shinny up the flagpole. I was a little afraid that he was going to fall and break his leg or something, but he didn't. For a principal, he was a good climber!

When he got to the top, we all recited the Pledge of Allegience with him. Then everybody let out a cheer.

When he was sliding down the flag-pole, Mr. Klutz got his foot caught in the rope that holds the flag. As he was trying to get his foot loose, his hand slipped and he fell. The next thing we knew, Mr. Klutz was hanging upside down from the flagpole. His Uncle Sam hat fell off.

Everybody gasped.

Mr. Klutz was just hanging there, halfway up the flagpole, like he was another flag or something. It would have been the funniest thing in the history of the world if we didn't honestly think Mr. Klutz was going to fall and land on his head.

"Help!" he shouted. "My foot is caught in the rope!"

"Quick! Get some pads from the gym

for him to land on!"
yelled Mrs. Roopy, the
school librarian.

"Call the fire
department!" yelled
Mrs. Cooney, the
nurse. Everybody was
running around like
crazy, and nobody
knew what to do. It
looked like Mr. Klutz
would have to just
hang there from the
flagpole all day.

"He'll figure a way
out of this," I told the

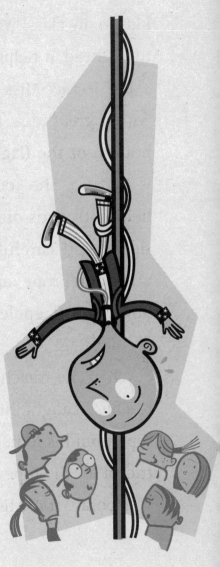

kids in my class. "When the blood rushes to his head, it helps him think."

But it was Miss Daisy who came up with a great idea. She went over to the bottom of the flagpole, where the rope is tied up. She took the knot out and held both ends of the rope tight. Then, slowly and carefully, she began to let out some rope and lower Mr. Klutz down the flagpole, just like he was a regular flag.

When he reached the bottom, the teachers caught him and loosened the rope from his foot. He was okay, he said, except for the rope burns on his leg.

"Hooray for Miss Daisy!" our class

cheered. After he was back on the ground, Mr. Klutz got up, brushed himself off, and walked up the front steps, like it was totally normal for a principal to hang upside down from a flagpole.

Mr. Klutz is nuts!

Mr. Klutz Is Getting Weirder

"Your Election Day essays were fantastic," Mr. Klutz told our class the next morning. He had a big bandage wrapped around his head. I'm guessing he must have either crashed his skateboard again or found another flagpole to fall off.

"Thank you!" we all said.

"But I was a little surprised by the number of spelling errors I found in them," he continued. "We need to improve the spelling at our school. So here is what I have decided to do. If you students can write out a list of one hundred thousand spelling words by Thanksgiving, I will dress up in a turkey costume and ride a pogo stick down Main Street."

"Yayyyyyyy!" everybody hollered.

"How about one thousand spelling words?" shouted Ryan.

"One hundred thousand spelling words," Mr. Klutz repeated. "That's my final offer. Take it or leave it. And every word must be spelled correctly. Have a nice day."

During lunch, I was sure that Andrea was going to start her list of spelling words just to show how smart she was. But she didn't. She just kind of sat there, picking at her food quietly.

"You know, I've been thinking," she finally said. "I'm beginning to wonder if something might be wrong with Mr. Klutz."

"Like what?" Emily asked.

"Maybe he has some kind of a personal problem."

"What do you mean?" Michael asked. "Mr. Klutz is a cool guy. Would you rather have a boring principal?"

"My mother is a psychologist," Andrea said, "and she says that people sometimes do weird things for reasons that are buried deep within their mind."

"What does that mean?" I asked.

"It means she thinks Mr. Klutz is nuts," said Michael.

"I didn't say that," Andrea went on. "All I'm saying is that maybe he didn't want to climb up the flagpole. Maybe he doesn't want to put on a turkey costume. Maybe he just wants people to like him, and the only way he knows to show that is to do nutty things. Maybe he's a sad, unhappy man. Maybe all he wants is a hug or something."

"That's the saddest story I ever heard!" Emily said. Then she started sobbing.

Me, Ryan, and Michael looked at one another. We all rolled our eyes up in our heads.

"Mr. Klutz is cool," Ryan said. "You're the one who has some kind of a personal problem, Andrea."

"Maybe Mr. Klutz is nuts," I said. "In fact, maybe he's not a principal at all. Did you ever think of that? Maybe Mr. Klutz escaped from a home for the criminally insane and he's just pretending to be a principal. Maybe our real principal is tied up to a chair in the dungeon down in the basement. My friend Billy told me—"

"There is no dungeon down in the basement," Emily insisted. "That's just one of those urban legends."

"Sure, that's just what he wants us to believe!" I told Emily. "He doesn't want us to know our real principal is tied up to a chair down there. He probably tortures him during summer vacation."

"I think you guys are nuts," Emily said.

"I'm worried about Mr. Klutz," Andrea said, biting her fingernails.

The Last Straw

I don't know if all that mumbo jumbo Andrea said was true or not. But I had to admit, Mr. Klutz was acting weirder and weirder.

After we finished the list of a hundred thousand spelling words and he pogo sticked down Main Street in a turkey

costume, he offered to paint his bald head orange if our school got the highest reading score in the county. We did, and he came into school the next day with an orange head.

Then he offered to let every kid in the school shoot a Ping-Pong ball at him if

we collected enough box tops to buy new computers for the school media center. We did that, too.

It was fun shooting Ping-Pong balls at Mr. Klutz, but even I was beginning to worry that there was something troubling him.

And then came the day when it was obvious to everybody that Mr. Klutz had gone off the deep end. It was at the end of morning announcements. Miss Daisy had stepped out of the room for a minute.

"Boys and girls," Mr. Klutz said over the loudspeaker, "winter vacation is coming up. If the students at our school read with their parents for one million minutes before school lets out, I will bungee-jump off the roof of the school dressed as Santa Claus!"

Me and Ryan and Emily and Andrea and Michael all looked at one another.

"That's the last straw!" Andrea said.

"There are plenty of straws," I told her. "Do you want me to get you one?"

"She means we can't take this anymore," Ryan told me.

"Is that what the last straw means?" I asked. "I always wondered what the last straw meant."

"At first I thought Mr. Klutz was just a funny guy," Andrea said seriously. "And he is. But he's also a deeply disturbed man. We've got to do something. If he keeps going like this, he might hurt himself again. Or even worse. If we don't stop him and something terrible happens, it would be our fault."

"I never thought of it that way," I said.

"What can we do?" Emily asked. "We're just kids."

"We have to have an intervention," Andrea said.

"What's that?" Ryan asked.

"It's when you sit down and tell somebody they have a problem," Andrea explained. "You force them to do something about it. My mother has to do interventions all the time."

"I'm not telling Mr. Klutz he has a problem," Ryan said.

"Me neither," agreed Michael.

"A.J., you started this whole thing," Andrea told me.

"I did not!"

"Sure you did. You were the one who gave him the idea to give out incentives for learning in the first place."

"That's true," the others agreed, looking at me like I was a criminal or something.

"All I did was hit a puck into Annette," I said.

"A.J., you've got to tell Mr. Klutz that if he bungee-jumps off the roof, we're not going to read one minute with our parents," Andrea said. "Two can play at this game. If he's going to do crazy things, we won't read any more books. We won't spell any more words. We won't do any more math problems. We won't learn anything."

I couldn't believe I was hearing this from Andrea. Her idea of having fun is to read the dictionary during recess. If she was willing to give up learning, she must be really serious about Mr. Klutz and his problems.

"But if we stop learning stuff," I protested, "we'll get dumber."

"In your case," Andrea told me, "that would be impossible."

A Hard Bargain

That afternoon we talked Miss Daisy into letting us go to Mr. Klutz's office for a meeting.

"We need to speak with Mr. Klutz," Andrea told the school secretary. "It's very important."

"It's a matter of life and death," Ryan said.

The secretary let us in. Mr. Klutz wasn't hanging from the ceiling or anything. He had on boxing gloves and he was punching his punching bag.

"May I help you kids?" he asked.

"Go ahead, A.J.," Andrea said, giving me a shove from behind.

"Mr. Klutz," I told him, "we have come to make a deal with you."

"Really? What kind of deal?"

"We decided that we will read a million minutes with our parents, but only if you don't jump off the roof."

"Only if I *don't* jump off the roof?" he

said, looking puzzled. "But I was going to jump off the roof as an incentive to encourage you to read with your parents at night."

"Well, we're going to read with our parents at night as an incentive to make you *not* jump off the roof."

"This is highly unusual," Mr. Klutz said. "I thought the principal should offer the students incentives, not the other way around."

"Your incentives have been getting more and more dangerous," Andrea told him. "We're afraid that you might get killed trying to help us learn."

"Yeah, and if you die, we'll feel guilty," I added.

"Now, let me get this straight," Mr. Klutz said. "I offered to jump off the roof if you read a million minutes at night with your parents. But you are saying you will only read a million minutes with your parents if I don't jump off the roof. Correct?"

"That's right," we said.

"What if I jumped off the basketball backboard in the gym into a swimming pool filled with foam blocks?" Mr. Klutz asked. "Would that be okay?"

"No!" we all said.

"Can I wear a suit made of bubble wrap and jump off the stage in the auditorium?"

"No!"

"No jumping off *anything*," Andrea insisted. "Not if you want us to read or write or do math. That's our final offer. Take it or leave it."

"You drive a hard bargain." Mr. Klutz sighed. "Okay, I won't jump."

"Have a nice day!" we all said.

Poor Mr. Klutz

The kids in the other grades were disappointed when they heard that Mr. Klutz had changed his mind about bungee-jumping off the roof of the school. Some of them were even mad at us for stopping him.

But when it was announced that there

would be a field trip to Water World if we reached our goal instead, they stopped being mad. Water World is probably the coolest water park in California.

A few days before vacation, the school

still hadn't reached our goal of a million minutes of reading with our parents. It looked like we were not going to make it in time.

Then Mr. Klutz got on the loudspeaker during morning announcements. "Students, there are three more nights to go before vacation," he told us. "I hate to do this, but if you don't reach your goal by Friday, the field trip to Water World will be called off and I will have no choice but to jump off the roof. Have a nice day."

After hearing that, everybody started reading with their parents like crazy. Even the sixth graders, who say that reading isn't cool. Everybody wanted to go to Water World. We reached a million minutes the day before school let out for vacation.

The field trip to Water World was awesome! They had about a hundred giant water slides, and in some of them you slid in the dark with laser beams shooting all over the place. We got to eat as much pizza and ice cream as we wanted.

They also had one of those giant, inflatable moon bounce thingies where you jump around like crazy inside it. After water sliding, eating all that junk food, and bouncing in the moon bounce, I thought I was going to throw up. It was the greatest day of my life.

Me and Ryan and Emily and Andrea and Michael went looking for Mr. Klutz to thank him. We found him standing next to the moon bounce thingy.

"Great party!" I told Mr. Klutz, and we all gave him a big hug. "If you ask me, you're the greatest principal in the history of the world."

"Thanks, A.J.!"

"See, you didn't need to bungee-jump off the school to make us learn," Andrea said.

"I guess not," Mr. Klutz said. He was looking up at the moon bounce. "But I was just thinking, if we brought one of these moon bounce things out to the front of the school, and I went up on the roof–"

"No!" we all yelled.

"I wouldn't even need a bungee cord–"

"No!"

"It's pretty soft–"

"No!"

I think it's going to be very hard work helping Mr. Klutz get over this need he has to do nutty things. Maybe by June, if the whole school works together, we might be able to cure him.

But it won't be easy.

Mrs. Roopy Is Loopy!

Dan Gutman

Pictures by
Jim Paillot

HarperTrophy®
An Imprint of HarperCollinsPublishers

To Emma

That Army Guy

My name is A.J. and I hate school.

If you ask me, they shouldn't teach kids how to read and write in school. They shouldn't teach math. They should teach kids how to do tricks on their bikes. That's what I want to learn! But my teacher, Miss Daisy, thinks reading and writing and math are really important for some reason.

Miss Daisy told us to write a story for homework and draw a picture to go with it. We read the stories out loud the next day in class.

Andrea Young, who thinks she knows everything, made up 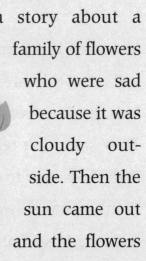 a story about a family of flowers who were sad because it was cloudy out-side. Then the sun came out and the flowers

2

got happy again.

It was a really dumb story, if you ask me. Flowers aren't happy or sad. They just sit there and do nothing. They don't even have families! But Miss Daisy kept telling Andrea how great the story was.

My story was about these giant man-eating monsters fighting on trick bikes in

outer space until they were all dead. I drew cool pictures to go with it. Emily, this girl with red hair, said my story was scary. But Emily thinks everything is scary.

Miss Daisy said I had a good imagination, but she asked me if next time I could try to write a story that didn't have so much violence in it.

"What's violent about giant man-eating monsters fighting on trick bikes in outer space?" I asked. Everybody laughed even though I didn't say anything funny.

Andrea said maybe I could have the man-eating monsters make up at the end of the story and tell each other they were sorry.

"Monsters don't apologize!" I said.

Everybody knows that. Andrea doesn't know anything about monsters.

We were arguing about it when all of a sudden some funny-looking guy marched into our classroom. He was all dressed up

in a fancy army uniform. He had a white wig on his head and a sword in his hand.

"To be prepared for war is the best way to keep the peace!" the army guy said. Then he marched out of the classroom.

"Who was that?" asked my friend Michael, who never ties his shoes no matter how many times he trips over the laces.

"Beats me," I said.

"Was that Principal Klutz?" asked my other friend Ryan, who sits next to me in the third row.

"I don't know who it was," Miss Daisy said, "but he is heading for the library. We'd better go check it out! Okay, second graders. Single file!"

The Librarian

Michael was the line leader. Andrea was the door holder. We went to the library, which is brand-new and didn't even exist last year when we were in first grade. They built it over the summer to replace the junky old library we used to have.

A library is the part in the school where they have hundreds of books that you can bring home with you. You don't even have to pay for them. And it's not even illegal! The only problem is you have to bring the books back after you're done reading them.

My friend Billy around the corner, who was in second grade last year, told me that if you don't bring back your library books on time, the librarian locks you in a dungeon under the school. I'm not sure I believe him.

"Our new librarian is Mrs. Roopy," Miss Daisy told us as we lined up in the hallway outside the library. "Everybody be on your best behavior so you'll make a good impression on her."

"I'm always on my best behavior," said

Andrea Young. She made a big dopey smile at Miss Daisy. Andrea is so annoying. If somebody told her to be on her worst behavior, she wouldn't know what to do.

When we went into the new library, we were shocked. Right in the middle of the room was a giant tree! It had a big tree house at the top near the ceiling and a ladder going up to it.

"What's with the tree?" I asked.

"Beats me," said Ryan. "How do you think they got it into the library?"

"Maybe it just grew in here over the summer," guessed Michael.

"Trees don't grow in libraries," said Andrea, as if she knows anything about trees.

"They must have built
it," said Emily.

"You don't build trees,
dumbhead," I told Emily,

and she looked all
hurt like she was
going to cry.

The tree was

really cool. Some of us started to climb it, but Miss Daisy said we had to get off because it was time for library period to start.

"Where's the new librarian?" Ryan

asked. We were all looking around, but we didn't see Mrs. Roopy anywhere.

Then, suddenly, that army guy with the wig poked his head out of the tree house. He came down the ladder. I think it was a he, anyway. He looked a little like a lady dressed like an army guy.

When he got to the bottom, the army guy with the wig stood all straight and proud at attention. He gave us a salute.

"Are you Mrs. Roopy?" I asked.

"Certainly not," the army guy said. "My name is George Washington. I am the first president of the United States and father of our country."

George Washington's Teeth

I'm no dumbhead. My mom told me that George Washington had wooden teeth. So this army guy with the wig couldn't be George Washington unless he had wooden teeth.

"If you're really George Washington, let's see your teeth," I said. The army guy with the wig reached into his pocket and pulled out a set of teeth. Then he wound a little thing on it and the teeth started chattering up and down in his hand.

Emily took one look at the teeth and ran out of the room crying. That girl cries at anything.

"Wow!" I said. "Maybe he is George Washington. Those teeth are cool! I wish I had wooden teeth."

"You can't fool me," Andrea Young said. "You're not George Washington. You're Mrs. Roopy, the new librarian, dressed up to look like George Washington. You're supposed to read stories to us and help us use the computers."

"Computers?" George Washington said, his forehead all wrinkly. "I don't know what you're talking about, young lady. This is the year 1790. Computers haven't been invented yet."

No matter what we said, the army guy with the wig insisted that he was really George Washington. He read us a story about when he was a boy and he chopped down a cherry tree. Then he showed us a bunch of books about the United States. All through library period, the army guy with the wig said that he was George Washington.

After a while, we started calling him George Washington.

"General Washington," I asked, "may I go to the bathroom?" Everybody laughed even though I didn't say anything funny. Kids think anything to do with bathrooms is funny. If you want to make your friends laugh, all you have to do is stick your face in their face and say either "bathroom" or "underwear." It works every time.

"I'm sorry," George Washington said. "This is the year 1790. Bathrooms have not been invented yet."

It wasn't an emergency or anything, so I waited. We were allowed to check out any book we wanted from the library. I took out a book about jet fighter planes because it had cool pictures in it.

For a president, this George Washington guy seemed to know a lot about finding books in the library and checking them out.

It was time to go to lunch. We all had to salute George Washington as we left the library.

"Hey, how come you chopped down that cherry tree, anyhow?" I asked him as we left the library.

"I cannot tell a lie," he said. "I needed some wood for my wooden teeth." Then he showed us his chattering teeth again. I'm still not sure if that army guy with the wig was George Washington or not. But he was weird.

Dumbheads

I took a seat in the lunchroom next to Ryan and Michael. Ryan stuck two of my carrot sticks in his nose, and I told him I'd give him a nickel if he ate them. He did, too. Me, I won't even eat carrot sticks *before* you stick them in your nose.

"Do you think that guy was really George Washington?" Ryan asked.

"I don't know," Michael said. "What do you think, A.J.?"

That's when Andrea Young leaned over from the next table and opened her big mouth.

"That wasn't George Washington, you dumbheads!" she said. "That was Mrs. Roopy wearing a powdered wig and an army uniform."

She may have been right, but I didn't want to admit it, because I hate her. Ryan took out a dollar bill from his backpack and looked at the picture of George Washington.

"He sure looked like George Washington," Ryan said.

"George Washington has been dead for like a hundred years!" Andrea said.

"Even if George Washington was still alive," Emily said, "I'm sure he would have more important things to do than come to our school and read us stories."

That's when it hit me. If that army guy was really Mrs. Roopy dressed up as George Washington, maybe Mrs. Roopy isn't a librarian at all!

"Maybe she's just pretending to be a librarian," I said, "just like she was pretending to be George Washington."

"Yeah!" Michael said. "Maybe she's a kidnapper and she's got our real librarian locked up in an empty warehouse at the edge of town. I saw that in a movie once."

"We've got to save her!" Emily said with

tears dribbling down her cheeks. Then she went running out of the room.

There was only one way to solve the problem. We cleaned off our trays and went back to our classroom to ask Miss Daisy if George Washington was really Mrs. Roopy in disguise.

"Don't be silly," Miss Daisy said. "As it turns out, Mrs. Roopy is absent today. She's home sick in bed. It must have been the real George Washington."

But what does Miss Daisy know? Everybody knows Miss Daisy is crazy.

Mrs. Roopy's Hero

Everybody in our class was excited before the next library period. We all wanted to see if George Washington would be there again.

When we got to the library, there was just this lady who looked a little bit like George Washington except she didn't have on an army uniform or a wig. She looked like a normal lady.

"Good morning, second graders," she said. "My name is Mrs. Roopy. I'm sorry I couldn't be here the other day for your library period."

"But you were here!" Ryan shouted.

"You must be

mistaken," Mrs. Roopy said. "I was home sick in bed."

"Can we see your wooden teeth again?" Michael asked.

"Yeah, can we?"

"Wooden teeth? Did you know that George Washington didn't have wooden teeth at all? His mouth was filled with cow's teeth."

"Ewww!" we all shouted.

I asked Mrs. Roopy, "Did the cow have George Washington's teeth in *her* mouth?"

"But that was you, wasn't it, acting like George Washington?" said Michael.

Mrs. Roopy's forehead got all wrinkly just like George Washington's did when we told him about computers. "I don't know what you're talking about."

We all looked at one another. I wasn't sure if she was telling the truth or not.

"If I were George Washington, would I have this?" Mrs. Roopy asked. Then she picked up her shirt and showed us her belly. She had a little tattoo of a heart right over her belly button. It was cool.

I had to admit that George Washington would never have a heart-shaped tattoo over his belly button. So maybe that army guy with the wig wasn't Mrs. Roopy after all.

"Let me show you around the library," Mrs. Roopy said. "Did you know that books can take you to places you have never been before? They help us explore our world. We have books here on just about every subject you can think of. This is the fiction section. Does anyone know the difference between fiction and nonfiction books?"

"Nonfiction books are books that are not fiction," Ryan said. "Because 'non' means *not*, like nonfat milk has no fat in it."

"And nonsense has no sense in it," Michael added.

"That's true," Mrs. Roopy said, "but there's a little more to it."

"Fiction is what you get when you rub two things together," I said.

Everybody laughed even though I didn't say anything funny.

"That's friction, A.J.," Andrea Young said. "Fiction is a made-up story, and non-fiction is based on facts."

"That's correct," said Mrs. Roopy, and she smiled at Andrea. I wished Andrea would shut up.

"Oh, who cares what the difference between fiction and nonfiction is?" I said. "All books are boring."

Everybody went "Ooooooh!" like I had said something really terrible.

"But everybody needs to know how to read, A.J.," Mrs. Roopy said.

"Not me," I said. "When I grow up, I'm going to be a trick bike rider because you don't have to know how to read to do tricks on a bike."

"Yeah, me too," said Michael and Ryan. We told Mrs. Roopy that, every day after school, me and Michael and Ryan ride our bikes together. I learned how to ride a two-wheeler in kindergarten. Now I can do a bunny hop off a bump, and I know the names of all the famous trick bike riders. I have posters of them all over the walls of my room.

"Gee, I don't know much about bicycle tricks, A.J.," Mrs. Roopy said. "But I've got posters of my hero on my walls at home too."

"Who is your hero, Mrs. Roopy?" Andrea asked.

"Melvil Dewey."

"Melvil Whoey?" I asked.

"Melvil Dewey was a very famous librarian," Mrs. Roopy said, and her eyes got all bright and sparkly and excited.

"Librarians aren't famous," I said.

"Melvil Dewey was," said Mrs. Roopy. "He invented the number system we use to find books in the library. If it weren't for Melvil Dewey, we would never be able to find anything."

"Wow!" Andrea Young said, as if she was really interested in that boring stuff.

"So if you want to find books about insects, you'd go to number 595," Mrs. Roopy said. "And if you want to find books about dinosaurs, you'd go to number 567. Libraries all over the world use the system that Melvil Dewey invented. Today we call it the Dewey decimal system."

"Did all the kids at his school make fun of him because his name was Melvil?" I asked. I know that if there was a kid named Melvil in our school, we would make fun of him constantly.

"I don't know," Mrs. Roopy said. "But would you like to hear a song I made up about Melvil Dewey?"

"Yeah!" we all shouted. Listening to songs had to be better than reading books.

Mrs. Roopy went into her office and came back with a guitar and one of those harmonica thingys you wear around your neck. She strummed a few chords to warm up.

"You may have heard a folktale about John Henry, the steel-drivin' man," Mrs. Roopy said. "Well, this is the story of Melvil Dewey, the book-sortin' man."

And then she started to sing. . . .

When Melvil Dewey was a little bitty
*   baby,*
The first words he said himself
Were "I've got to get these books off the
*   floor*
And put them on the shelf. . . ."

Mrs. Roopy sang the whole song and played her guitar and harmonica, too. It was a pretty cool song. This Melvil Dewey guy had a race with a computer to see who could sort books the fastest. Melvil won the race, but right after he sorted the last book, he dropped dead right on the floor of the library. It was cool.

At the end of the song, Andrea Young got up and gave Mrs. Roopy a standing ovation, so we all had to get up too.

"That's the saddest story I ever heard in my life," Emily said, wiping tears from her eyes.

At the end of the period, Mrs. Roopy asked us if we had any questions about how to use the library.

"Is it true that if we don't return our library books on time you lock us in a dungeon under the school?" I asked. Everybody laughed even though I didn't say anything funny.

"Don't be silly," Mrs. Roopy said. "The dungeon is on the third floor." I think she was telling a joke, but I'm not sure.

Johnny Applesauce

When we came into the library the next time, a guy with a long beard came down the ladder from the tree house, wearing blue-jean overalls. He was carrying a shovel and a big sack. He had no shoes on his feet, but he was wearing a pot on his head. He looked funny, and he looked a lot like Mrs. Roopy to me.

"Mrs. Roopy, why are you wearing a pot on your head?" I asked.

"Roopy?" the guy said in a funny voice. "You young 'uns must be confusin' me with some other feller. My name is Johnny Appleseed. It's the year 1800. I travel from

town to town plantin' apple trees most everywhere I wander."

"You are not Johnny Appleseed!" Andrea called out. "You're Mrs. Roopy!"

"Ain't never heard of no Roopy," the guy said, making his forehead all wrinkly. "Appleseed's the name. Plantin' apple trees is my game. This here's a darn big country, and I reckon folks are gonna need a heap of apples."

No matter what we said, we couldn't convince the bearded guy with the pot on his head that he wasn't Johnny Appleseed. He read us a story about Johnny Appleseed and told us lots of stuff about apples.

"Did you know that folks have been eatin' apples for thousands of years?" Johnny Appleseed told us.

"They should chew faster," I said, and everybody laughed.

Then Johnny Appleseed took us outside and helped us plant a real apple tree near the playground. Before we went back into school, we had apples for snack.

I can understand why he planted all those apple trees. I can understand why he was dressed funny. But what I don't understand is why he wore a pot on his head. That Johnny Applesauce guy was weird.

When we got back to class, I told Miss

Daisy all about what happened during library period.

"Do you still think books are boring, A.J.?" she asked me.

"Yes," I said.

One Small Step for Man

By this time, we weren't sure if Johnny Appleseed and George Washington had been to our school, or if it was just Mrs. Roopy dressed up in funny costumes. But we were sure of one thing.

Mrs. Roopy is loopy!

"We have to have proof," Michael said.

"My father is a policeman, and he said that if you want to be sure of something, you have to have proof. He always says the proof is in the pudding."

"What does pudding have to do with it?" I asked.

"Beats me," said Michael.

"Your dad is weird," I said.

"How are we going to prove that Mrs. Roopy is dressing up in funny costumes?" Ryan asked.

"We'll get her fingerprints!" Michael said, all excited. "That's what my dad does. Everybody in the whole world has different fingerprints. If we get Johnny Appleseed's fingerprints and then we get

Mrs. Roopy's fingerprints, I can have my dad test them. If they are the same fingerprints, then that will be proof that Mrs. Roopy was just pretending to be Johnny Appleseed!"

Me and Ryan agreed that Michael was a genius. The next time we had library, we brought a juice box with us, so we could get Mrs. Roopy's fingerprints.

But when we came into the library, all the lights were out and the shades were down. It was really dark. At first we thought the library was closed. Then we heard a noise. It came from the top of the tree house. We all looked up.

Somebody was coming down the

ladder. Whoever it was had on a spacesuit and was moving in slow motion. Some music began playing over the loudspeaker. "The *Eagle* . . . has landed," the astronaut said. Finally the astronaut reached the bottom rung of the ladder. It was hard to see a face through the space helmet.

"It's got to be Mrs. Roopy!" Andrea said.

"I'm not Mrs. Roopy," the astronaut said. "My name is Neil Armstrong. It is 1969. I am about to

become the first human being to set foot on the moon."

Slowly Neil Armstrong put one foot on the floor of the library.

"That's one small step for man, one giant leap for mankind," he said.

We tried to convince Neil Armstrong that he was really Mrs. Roopy dressed in a spacesuit, but he kept saying he had never heard of anyone named Roopy. Neil Armstrong spent the rest of the period showing us books about the moon and the sun and the stars and outer space. It was almost not boring, but not quite.

"Would you like some juice, Mr. Armstrong?" Michael asked, holding out the juice box.

"No thank you," Neil Armstrong said. "I've got to be getting back to Earth now. And I believe you have to go back to Miss Daisy's class."

Then he climbed up the ladder and into the tree house. Michael was disappointed that he didn't get Neil Armstrong's fingerprints.

When we got back to class, I told Miss Daisy all about Neil Armstrong stepping on the surface of the moon for the first time.

"Wow, that sounds exciting!" Miss Daisy said. "Do you still think books are boring, A.J.?"

"Yes," I said.

Nursery Rhyme Week

The only way to prove that Mrs. Roopy was dressing up in silly costumes and pretending to be other people would be to get her fingerprints. Me and Ryan and Michael were determined to get them the next time we had library.

"When do we have library this week?" we asked Miss Daisy.

"Oh, there is no library this week," she said. "The whole school is celebrating Nursery Rhyme Week in our classrooms."

"Oh man!" I said. "We wanted to go to the library."

"Yeah," agreed Michael and Ryan.

Miss Daisy looked all surprised. She put her hand on my forehead the way my mom does when she thinks I have a fever.

"Are you sick, A.J.?" Miss Daisy said. "There must be something wrong with you if you want to go to the library. Didn't you say all books are boring?"

"They are," I said. "I just want proof that Mrs. Roopy was pretending to be George Washington, Johnny Appleseed, and Neil Armstrong. We have to get her fingerprints."

"Oh, don't be silly," Miss Daisy said. "Mrs. Roopy is a perfectly normal lady."

Miss Daisy took out a big fat Mother Goose book. She opened it and was about to start reading when this weird-looking girl skipped into the classroom. She was all dressed up in a puffy dress and she was holding a big cane.

"It's Mrs. Roopy!" we all shouted.

"I'm not Mrs. Roopy," the girl said. "My name is Little Bo Peep. I seem to have lost my sheep. Do you know where I can find them?"

"Nope," everybody said.

"Maybe they're in the dungeon on the

third floor," I said.

Michael tried to get her fingerprints, but Little Bo Peep went skipping out of the classroom before he could get a juice box.

"That was weird," Emily said.

"What kind of a name is Peep, anyway?" I asked.

Miss Daisy read us some nursery rhymes from the Mother Goose book. What kind of a name is Goose, anyway?

After a while, this other girl came running into our classroom. She was holding a bucket in her hand.

"It's Mrs. Roopy again!" we all shouted.

"Who are you now, Mrs. Roopy?" Emily asked.

"I'm not Mrs. Roopy," the girl said. "My name is Jill. I ran up a hill with my friend Jack to fetch a pail of water. But Jack fell down and broke his crown. I went running after him, but now I have no idea where he is. Have you seen him?"

"Nope," everybody said.

"Try the dungeon on the third floor," I said.

"You must be thirsty from all that running," Michael said. "Have some juice."

"No time for that," Jill said. "I've got to find Jack." And then she ran out of the classroom.

After lunch we were at recess out in the playground when we noticed somebody sitting at the edge of the grass under a tree. We all ran over to investigate. It was Mrs. Roopy, of course, dressed up in another silly costume.

"Are you Little Bo Peep again?" Emily asked.

"Heavens, no!" said Mrs. Roopy. "My

name is Little Miss Muffet. It's a lovely day, so I thought I'd just sit on this tuffet and eat some curds and whey."

"What's a tuffet?" I asked, trying to peek under Miss Muffet.

"What's a curd?" asked Ryan.

"Yuck," Michael said. "Curds sound disgusting!"

"I'm going to throw up," Ryan said. "That's even worse than what they serve in the cafeteria!"

"Wouldn't you rather have a peanut butter and jelly sandwich?" I asked.

Andrea and Emily came over while we were talking with Little Miss Muffet. Andrea started to tell us what curds and whey and tuffets were, but she never got to finish. This obviously fake spider came down from the tree over Miss Muffet's head. She took one look at it and ran back to school. Michael didn't even have the chance to get her fingerprints.

That lady is weird.

It went on like that for the rest of the week. All these nursery rhyme characters kept popping up with no warning

all over the school.

"Who are you now?" we would ask.

"I'm an old woman in a shoe. I have so many children I don't know what to do."

"Maybe you should put some of them in the dungeon on the third floor," I said.

In the next few days we were visited by Wee Willie Winkie, Georgie Porgie, Tommy Tucker, Simple Simon, Peter Peter Pumpkin Eater, and some guy named Jack who kept jumping over a candlestick for no reason at all. I guess it was the same Jack that girl Jill was looking for.

It was nonstop all week! I can't say for sure, but I'm pretty sure at least some of those nursery-rhyme characters were actually Mrs. Roopy.

Mrs. Roopy's Problem

Something was wrong with Andrea. She wasn't raising her hand in class every second. She wasn't bragging to everybody how much she knew about everything. She wasn't pestering me like she usually did. It was like she was sick or something.

"What's the matter, Andrea?" Emily asked her during recess.

"I'm worried about Mrs. Roopy," Andrea said. "I'm afraid she might have a serious personal problem."

"You're the one with the serious personal problem," I said. "Mrs. Roopy is like the coolest lady in the history of the world. Would you rather have some boring librarian who didn't dress up in

costumes or anything and all she did was read boring books to us?"

"No, but my mother is a psychologist," Andrea said. "She told me that some sick people have more than one personality. Like one minute they think they are one person, and a minute later they actually think they are somebody completely different. The whole time they actually think they are all these people. I'm afraid that Mrs. Roopy might have this problem. She can't tell the difference between the real world and fantasy."

"Wow," Michael said. "That sounds pretty serious."

"We've got to help her!" Emily said.

"Yeah," I said. "A librarian who doesn't know the difference between fiction and nonfiction is in big trouble."

"But what can we do?" Ryan asked.

We all put on our thinking caps. Well, not really. There's no such thing as a thinking cap. But you know what I mean.

After a good long think, I came up with a great plan.

The Evidence

There were five minutes left in recess. Ryan, Michael, Andrea, Emily, and I sneaked in from the playground through the door to the library.

"Shhhhh!" I said as we tiptoed into the library. "Follow me."

Lucky for us, the library was empty. Mrs. Roopy was probably eating lunch in the teachers' room.

On our hands and knees, we made our way past the nonfiction books to Mrs. Roopy's office. The door was unlocked. I opened it.

"We're going to get caught," Emily said.

"We're going to be kicked out of school and thrown in jail for the rest of our lives."

"In here," I said, ignoring Emily. "This is where we'll find the evidence."

We were inside Mrs. Roopy's office. I wanted to turn the light on, but Michael told me that when his father is doing a secret investigation, he never turns the lights on. We tried to see the best we could with the light that came in through the window.

"Do you see any evidence?" Michael said.

"Not yet."

It was just a bunch of boring stuff.

Pictures of Mrs. Roopy's daughter. Papers. Videos. Junk. No evidence at all.

"Let's get out of here," Emily said. "I'm scared."

"Not yet," I said.

There was a closet by the corner. I pulled the handle. It wasn't locked.

And there, inside the closet, was all the evidence we would ever need. George Washington's uniform. Little Bo Peep's dress. Johnny Appleseed's overalls. Neil Armstrong's spacesuit. Every single costume Mrs. Roopy had been wearing was hanging right there in the closet.

"This is the proof!" Michael said. "All those people were just Mrs. Roopy dressed up in costumes."

"I told you so," said Andrea.

"You did not!" I said.

"Did too!" she said.

"Oh, you think you know everything!" I said. "Well, you're not so smart!"

That's when the light flicked on. It was Mrs. Roopy, standing in the doorway looking at us.

"What's the meaning of this?" she asked.

She had her hands on her hips, so we knew she was mad. For some reason, grown-ups always put their hands on their hips when they are mad.

"I had nothing to do with it!" Andrea said. "It was all A.J.'s idea!"

Everybody was looking at me. I had to think fast. I didn't want to spend the rest of my life in jail.

I grabbed George Washington's uniform out of the closet.

"What's the meaning of . . . *this*?" I said, holding up the costume. "You told us you were home sick in bed and George Washington was here instead of you. How do you explain the fact that George

Washington's uniform is in your closet? Huh?"

We all turned to look at Mrs. Roopy.

She just stood there for a moment and then . . . she broke down crying. She was sobbing and big tears were running down her face. It was so sad that we all gathered around her and gave her a hug. Emily was crying too.

"This is horrible!" Mrs. Roopy said, wiping her eyes with a tissue.

"You'll be okay, Mrs. Roopy," Andrea said. "We'll get you some help."

"No, it's horrible!" Mrs. Roopy cried. "George Washington must have left his uniform in my closet when he was here.

Do you know what this means?"

"What?"

"It means George Washington is running around somewhere with no clothes on!"

Just Admit It!

It was no use. Even after we proved to Mrs. Roopy that she was dressing up as all these characters, she still wouldn't admit it.

"Mrs. Roopy is in denial," Andrea said when we got back to the classroom. "I'll bet you don't know what that means, A.J."

"Sure I know what 'denial' means," I said. "It's that river in Africa."

"Not the Nile, dumbhead! Denial! It means she can't admit to herself that she has a problem."

"So what are we supposed to do now?" Michael asked.

"There's only one thing we can do," Andrea said. "We've got to tell Mr. Klutz."

Mr. Klutz is the principal, which means he is like the king of the school. One time I got into trouble and was sent to Mr. Klutz's office. When I got there, he didn't punish me. He gave me a candy bar. Mr. Klutz is nuts!

We told Miss Daisy that we had to speak with Mr. Klutz and that it was a matter of life and death. She called the office and in a few minutes Mr. Klutz arrived.

Mr. Klutz has no hair at all. We told him all about the crazy things Mrs. Roopy had been doing and how Andrea's mother is a psychologist and she thinks Mrs. Roopy might have a big problem.

"We're really worried about her," Emily said.

"Hmmm, this sounds pretty serious," Mr.

Klutz said. "Maybe we'd better go have a little chat with Mrs. Roopy."

Mr. Klutz led us down the hall to the library. When

we got there, Mrs. Roopy was lying on the floor under the tree house. She was holding her head like it had been hit. Not only that, but Mrs. Roopy was really fat. It looked like she had gained about a million hundred pounds!

"What happened, Mrs. Roopy?" Michael asked. "Are you okay?"

"Mrs. Roopy? Who's that?" Mrs. Roopy said. "My name is Humpty Dumpty. I was sitting on that wall up there, and I had a great fall."

"Don't tell me," Andrea said. "All the king's horses and all the king's men couldn't put you back together again. Right?"

"How did you know?" Mrs. Roopy asked.

"You're not Humpty Dumpty!" Andrea said. "You're Mrs. Roopy, our librarian! Just admit it!"

"It doesn't matter who it is," Mr. Klutz said. "There has been an injury. I need to write a report and give it to the Board of Education."

"You can give it to me," I told Mr. Klutz.

"I'm bored of education."

Everybody laughed even though I didn't say anything funny. Mr. Klutz said he had to go call a doctor for Humpty Dumpty. Mrs. Roopy got up off the floor and dusted herself off.

"Wait a minute," I said. "I have a question."

"Yes, A.J.?" asked Mrs. Roopy.

"Your name is Humpty Dumpty, right?"

"Right."

"What I want to know is, why did your parents name you Humpty? I mean, if their last name was already Dumpty, they could have named you John or Jim or Joe or something normal. But they had to go and name you Humpty?"

"Well, actually, Humpty is just my nick-name," Mrs. Roopy said. "My real name is Lumpy."

"Lumpy Dumpty?" I said.

"Yes," said Mrs. Roopy. "So you can see why I'd rather be called Humpty."

Andrea was getting all angry now. Mrs. Roopy was simply not going to admit she wasn't Humpty Dumpty.

"Nursery Rhyme Week is over, Mrs. Roopy!" Andrea said. "You can be your-self. You can stop pretending to be other people."

"Don't you like nursery rhymes?" asked Mrs. Roopy.

"Sure I do," Andrea said. "But enough is enough!"

"I hate nursery rhymes!" I said. "Nursery rhymes are dumb. I'm sick of nursery rhymes. Nursery rhymes are boring."

Humpty, I mean, Mrs. Roopy, looked hurt.

"Everything is boring to you, A.J.," she said sadly. "I've tried so hard not to bore you. Please. Tell me. What is not boring to you?"

I put on my thinking cap (well, not really) and tried real hard to think of something that wasn't boring.

"Trick bikes," I said. "Trick bikes aren't boring."

The Proof

It was the middle of our afternoon snack time. I traded my pretzel sticks with Ryan for his cup of chocolate pudding. Suddenly I heard somebody yelling down the hallway.

"Watch out! Coming through! Out of the way!"

"I wonder what that could be," said Miss Daisy.

The yelling got louder. Everybody in the class turned around just in time to see somebody ride into our classroom on a trick bike.

It was Mrs. Roopy! She was wearing sunglasses, knee pads, elbow pads, and a floppy black T-shirt that said "Bikers 4 Books." She had combed her hair to make it stick up all spiky.

"Hey, dudes!" she said as she skidded to a stop right in front of my desk. "I just landed an awesomely tweaked tailwhip with a Superman seat grab to a toothpick grind. You should have seen it! It was really sick!"

Everybody put down their snacks and gathered around my desk to look at Mrs. Roopy's cool bike.

"I didn't know you knew so much about trick biking, Mrs. Roopy," I said.

"I'm not Mrs. Roopy," Mrs. Roopy said.

"I'm a professional trick biker!"

"You are not!" we all hollered. "You're Mrs. Roopy, the librarian!"

"Am not!"

"Are too!"

"It certainly looks like a trick biker to me," said Miss Daisy.

That's when I came up with the most genius idea in the history of the world. Mrs. Roopy's tattoo! I remembered that she had a picture of a heart on her belly button!

"You're Mrs. Roopy," I said, grabbing the bottom of her T-shirt, "and I can prove it!"

"Oh, stop that!" Mrs. Roopy giggled. "I'm ticklish!"

When I yanked at her shirt, three books fell out. One of them hit my snack on my desk. The cup of chocolate pudding went flying. It splashed all over Mrs. Roopy's tummy. It almost covered up the tattoo of a heart, but we could still see it.

"It's Mrs. Roopy!" Michael shouted. "The proof is in the pudding!"

"Hey!" Ryan shouted. "Check out these books!" Ryan picked up the books that had dropped on the floor. They were books about trick biking! One of the books showed how to do tricks, and the other two were about famous trick bikers. Cool!

"I didn't know they made books about trick biking," Ryan said.

"So that's how you know so much about trick biking, Mrs. Roopy!" I said.

"I don't know what you're talking about," Mrs. Roopy said. "I'm a professional trick biker."

"Can I check these books out of the

library?" asked Michael.

"No, I get them first," Ryan said.

"Hey, I was the one who found them," I said.

Miss Daisy grabbed all the books.

"Gee, I don't know, A.J.," she said. "You said that reading was boring, so you probably wouldn't want to read these books."

"Yes I would!" I shouted. "Pleeeeease?"

"Well, okay," Miss Daisy said as she handed each of us one of the trick bike books. "But if you don't bring these back on time, Mrs. Roopy is going to lock you in the dungeon on the third floor."

We all looked at Mrs. Roopy.

"Later, dudes!" she said. And with that,

Mrs. Roopy went pedaling out into the hallway.

I feel sorry for Mrs. Roopy. She is the loopiest librarian I've ever met. I think she's got a big problem. We're going to do all we can to help her. But it won't be easy.

MS. Hannah Is Bananas!

Dan Gutman

Pictures by
Jim Paillot

HarperTrophy®
An Imprint of HarperCollinsPublishers

To Emma

I Hate
Andrea Young

"Miss Daisy! A.J. hit me!"

"I did not," I said.

"He did too! He bumped his elbow against my elbow!"

Andrea Young is so annoying. I barely touched her stupid elbow. She was moaning and holding her arm like an elephant stepped on it.

1

I wish an elephant would step on her *head*. Andrea has been bothering me since we were little kids. And that's a long time, because now we're in second grade.

"I saw A.J. do it, Miss Daisy," said Emily. She is Andrea's friend and is just as annoying. But in a different way.

"Am I going to have to send anyone to Mr. Klutz's office?" Miss Daisy asked.

Mr. Klutz is the principal, and that means he is like the king of the school.

"No," me and Andrea said.

"Good, because it's time for us to go to art class. I don't want you to miss it. Our art teacher, Ms. Hannah, is really nice, and I'm sure she has some fun activities planned for you."

"Art?" I said. "I hate art."

"Oh, you hate everything, A.J.," said Andrea, who thinks she knows everything.

It just so happens that I do *not* hate everything. I don't hate football. I don't hate skateboarding. I don't hate trick biking. I don't hate monster movies. Especially when the monsters crush cars and stuff. But I do hate school, and I especially hate Andrea.

"I *love* art," Andrea announced, like anybody really cared. She took out a big art box she had brought from home. It had crayons and colored pencils and other stuff in it. "When I grow up, I want to be an artist. My mom thinks I'm really creative. I like to create things."

"She should create an empty space where she is right now," I whispered to my friend Ryan, who sits in the row next to me.

"Hahahaha!" Ryan laughed, but Miss Daisy made a mean face at him and he shut up.

"Let's go, second graders!" she said. "Single file to the art room. Ms. Hannah is waiting for us."

Drawing pictures is for babies, if you ask me. And art is stupid.

Finger Painting with Ms. Hannah

Emily was the door holder. My friend Michael who never ties his shoes was the line leader. The art room was all the way on the other side of the school. We had to walk about a million hundred miles to get there. Michael told Miss Daisy it was like walking across the Grand Canyon, so she let us take drinks from the water fountain outside the art room.

That's where Ms. Hannah was standing. She was the funniest-looking lady I ever saw. She was wearing a dress that looked like it was made from a bunch of different-colored washcloths that were sewed together. On her hands were these big mittens that my mom uses when she has to take hot dishes out of the oven.

Ms. Hannah looked weird.

"Good morning, second graders," she said as we filed into the art room. "Do you like my new dress? It's made from

used pot holders that I bought on eBay. I stitched them together."

Ms. Hannah spun around so we could get the full effect of her new dress.

"It's beautiful!" Andrea said. She is always complimenting (that's a big word!) grown-ups on everything. Andrea was born old. Personally I thought it was the stupidest-looking dress in the history of the world. I went to sit with my friends Michael and Ryan, but Miss Daisy stopped us.

She told Ms. Hannah that *certain* people should not sit next to other *certain* people. I knew what that meant.

"Boy-girl-boy-girl," Miss Daisy said,

pointing to where we should sit. I had to sit at a table between Andrea and her crybaby friend Emily.

Miss Daisy gave each of us a name tag to wear so Ms. Hannah would know our names. Then she told Ms. Hannah she would be in the teachers' lounge in case there was any trouble.

The teachers' lounge is where the teachers go when they don't have to teach.

I've never been in there. No kid has *ever* been in there in the history of the world, because kids aren't allowed inside. The teachers' lounge is like a secret clubhouse for teachers only.

My friend Billy from around the corner who was in second grade last year told me that they have big parties in the teachers' lounge all day long. He said the teachers dance around and play Pin the Tail on the Donkey and eat cake and take target practice with BB guns. Then they try and think up new punishments to give us kids when we misbehave.

That sounds cool. Maybe when I grow up, I'll be a teacher so I can hang out in the teachers' lounge all day and have fun.

After we sat at our tables, Ms. Hannah

took off her pot-holder mitts and picked up a piece of black paper.

"Can anyone tell me what *this* is?" she asked.

Any dumbhead knows that. I raised my hand, and she called on me. "It's a piece of black paper," I said. "Duh!"

"It *could* be a piece of black paper, A.J.," Ms. Hannah said. "But maybe it's a black cat in a coal mine. Maybe it's a crow flying in the middle of the night."

It was a trick question! I *hate* trick questions! My ears felt like they were on fire. I didn't look at anybody, but I knew everybody was looking at me and laughing to themselves.

It wasn't fair! That stupid thing was a

plain old piece of black paper, and every-body knew it.

"It looks like a piece of black paper to me," my friend Ryan said. Whew! I knew I could count on Ryan. I turned around and gave him the thumbs-up sign.

"I want you to open your imaginations, second graders," Ms. Hannah said. "Art is everything and everywhere! It's all around us! We are all artists. A dentist is an artist. Your mouth is your dentist's canvas. A man fixing a roof is an artist. You can be an artist too."

Not me, I thought to myself. Art is stupid.

Ms. Hannah put a big sheet of newspa-per in front of each of us to cover the table. She took a bunch of old T-shirts out of the closet and gave one to every-body to wear so we wouldn't get paint all over ourselves. Then she put paint in the middle of all the tables and gave each of us a piece of white paper.

"Today we are going to finger paint," she said.

"I'm not painting *my* fingers," I said. Some of the kids laughed, even though I didn't say anything funny.

"You silly dumbhead," Andrea said. "Finger painting is when you use your fingers to paint pictures."

I knew that. Andrea thinks she knows everything.

"What should we paint?" Emily asked

Ms. Hannah.

"Anything you like! Express your creativity. Paint what you love."

"I love butterflies," Andrea said. "I'm going to finger paint a picture of a happy family of butterflies."

"I'm going to finger paint a picture of a tree in a forest where your butterflies can live," said Emily.

"I'm going to finger paint a picture of a tree falling in a forest and crushing a family of happy butterflies until they are dead," I said.

"That's mean!" Emily said. She looked like she was going to cry, like she does at every stupid little thing.

"Hey, I'm just expressing myself," I said.

I turned around and saw that Ryan was finger painting an airplane. Michael was finger painting a house. Everybody was hard at work finger painting.

The finger paint looked yucky to me. I didn't really want to get it all over my hands. It was disgusting. I just sat there watching everybody finger paint. My piece of paper was the only one that was perfectly white.

"Why aren't you finger painting, A.J.?" Emily whispered to me.

"Mind your own business, dumbhead."

"Ms. Hannah!" Andrea called out. "A.J. isn't finger painting."

Andrea is a big tattletale. She stuck out her tongue at me as Ms. Hannah came over to our table.

"A.J., you haven't finger painted a thing," Ms. Hannah said.

I didn't know what to do. I didn't know what to say. I had to think fast. "I did too finger paint something," I said. "This is a picture of a white polar bear. He's playing in the snow. *White* snow. And he's eating . . . vanilla ice cream!"

All the kids were looking at me. Ms. Hannah was looking at me. I was afraid she was going to yell or go get Miss Daisy from the teachers' lounge to take me to the principal's office.

"Very nice finger painting, A.J.!" Ms. Hannah said with a big smile on her face. "That's using your creativity!"

Hahaha! I stuck my tongue out at Andrea. She folded her arms across her front all mad-like.

It was great. It was not only great. It was the greatest moment in the history of the world. This was the next best thing to an elephant stepping on Andrea's head.

Pretty soon it was time to clean up. Ms. Hannah taught us a song about cleaning up. The words were, "Clean up, clean up, everybody everywhere. Clean up, clean up, everybody do their share."

It was a pretty dumb song, and me and Michael and Ryan changed the words to "Clean up, clean up, even in your underwear."

Any time anybody says a word that rhymes with "air," you should always change it to "underwear." Everybody will laugh. Believe me, this works *every* time.

Ms. Hannah peeled the sheets of painty newspaper off our desks and stuck them on a ball that was sitting on the windowsill. The ball was about the size of a beach ball.

"What are you doing, Ms. Hannah?" Michael asked.

"I'm making a newspaper ball," she said.

"Why?" we all asked.

"Old newspapers with paint all over them can be art. This is my art. Like I said, art is every-where. And this way, nothing goes to waste. I don't like waste. If you look around, you'll see that I don't even have a garbage can in here."

We looked around. It was true. There was no garbage can in the art room. Ms. Hannah didn't need a garbage can, because she never threw anything away. "That reminds me," Ms. Hannah said. "For our next class, I would like you all to bring in things from home that your parents were planning to throw away."

"What for?"

"So we can make them into art."

I was still looking around for a garbage can. She had to have a garbage can *somewhere*. Everybody needs a garbage can.

"It's a shame when people throw things

away," Ms. Hannah said. "Everything in the world is beautiful. Everything can be used to make some kind of art."

"Well, I just blew my nose," I said, holding out a tissue. "Does that make my boogers artistic?" Everybody laughed even though I didn't say anything funny. Ms. Hannah took my tissue and stuck it to her big newspaper ball.

It was disgusting.

Weird People

In the lunchroom I got to sit next to Ryan and Michael. I gave my apple to Ryan, and he gave me his yogurt with sprinkles in it.

"Ms. Hannah is weird," I said.

"Artists are always weird," Ryan said. "My mom has a friend who's an artist, and she's really weird. My mom says that's because artists are creative."

"Your mom is weird," Michael said.

"Lots of people are weird," I told them. "That doesn't make them creative. Some people are just weird, and they're not creative at all. And some people are creative, and they're not at all weird."

"You're weird, A.J.," Ryan said.

"Anybody who wears a dress made of pot holders is weird," Michael said.

"Art teachers are supposed to dress funny," I said.

"If my dad dressed like that, he'd be fired," Ryan said.

"Your dad is a businessman," Michael told Ryan. "He has to wear a tie around his neck every day. It doesn't do anything. It's just a piece of cloth that hangs around his neck. If you ask me, that's pretty weird."

"Yeah," I said, "which is weirder, wearing a dress made out of pot holders, or wearing a piece of cloth around your neck for no reason at all?"

"They're both weird," Ryan said.

"All grown-ups are weird, especially art teachers," said Michael.

"Ms. Hannah is weird, even for an art teacher," I said. I noticed that Andrea and Emily at the next table were listening to us. I knew they were listening because they kept shaking their heads and rolling their eyes and snickering at us.

"Maybe Ms. Hannah isn't really an art teacher at all," I said, just loud enough so the girls would hear it. "Did you ever think about that? Maybe she's just pretending to be an art teacher."

"Yeah!" Michael said. "Maybe Ms. Hannah is a thief, and she's trying to steal all our garbage and take over the world. Stuff like that happens in comic books all the time."

"Maybe our real art teacher was kidnapped, and she's tied up to a chair in the teachers' lounge," Ryan said.

"And the teachers are shooting BB guns at her," I added.

"We've got to save her!" Emily suddenly said. There were tears running down her cheeks. Then she got up and went running out of the room.

Me and Ryan and Michael laughed our heads off. That Emily is such a crybaby.

"You boys are weird," Andrea said.

What a Mess!

The next time we had art class, the newspaper ball that Ms. Hannah had been making was *huge*! It was about as high as a desk. Everybody wanted to touch it. Everyone except for me, that is. I remembered that somewhere inside that ball was my booger.

The art room was filled with all kinds of junk kids brought in from home. There were old musical instruments, broken toys, soda cans, plastic wrap, and all kinds of garbage. You should have seen it! Some kid brought in a tennis racquet with no strings.

"What a mess!" Emily said.

"If my bedroom looked like this, my mom would go crazy," Michael said. "You should throw half this stuff in the garbage, Ms. Hannah."

"Oh dear, no," she said. "I don't like to throw things away. In fact, at home the garbagemen bring *me* garbage so I can use it in my art. When I have a day off, I go to junkyards looking for treasures."

Ms. Hannah is bananas!

She had some sticky glue that sticks to everything. She told us to make a sculpture out of the junk kids brought in from home.

"Express yourself!" Ms. Hannah said. "Show your creativity! Remember, art is everywhere. Art is light. Art is air. Even things that are invisible can be art."

Michael started making a robot out of toilet paper tubes. Emily made a doll out of buttons.

I didn't know what to make. I think I'm just not very artistic. I didn't feel like gluing a bunch of junk together. Ms. Hannah walked around looking at everyone's sculptures and telling them how wonderful they were. I hoped Ms. Hannah wouldn't come over to me.

"A.J. isn't making a sculpture," Andrea said, and she stuck her tongue out at me. I hate her.

"Why aren't you making anything, A.J.?"

I didn't know what to do. I didn't know what to say. I had to think fast. "I did make a sculpture," I said. "This is an invisible sculpture. I call it 'The Invisible Sculpture.'"

"Very clever, A.J.!" Ms. Hannah said. "That's using your creativity!"

I stuck out my tongue at Andrea.

"I have an announcement, second

grade," Ms. Hannah said after clean-up time. "Mr. Klutz has agreed to sponsor a big art contest. There will be a prize for the winner in each grade."

"What's the prize?" Ryan asked.

"A gift certificate for a hundred dollars to an art supply store."

Everybody went "ooh" and "wow." It didn't seem like a great prize to me. I don't like art. What would I do with a bunch of art supplies?

Ms. Hannah said we had to create our artwork at home and bring it in two weeks later if we wanted to be in the contest.

"You can make anything you like," Ms. Hannah said, "and use whatever materials you want. Freely express yourselves!

Creativity is the most important thing."

"Can we just draw pictures?" Michael asked.

"Of course!" said Ms. Hannah.

"I hope I win," I heard Andrea whisper to Emily. "I'm going to make a sculpture with butterflies."

I hate her. I wonder if there are poisonous butterflies that bite people.

"So who thinks they might enter the contest?" asked Ms. Hannah. Everybody raised their hands except for me.

"What about you, A.J.?"

I didn't say anything. But I'll tell you what I was thinking: I hate art! Art is stupid!

5

The Secret of the Teachers' Lounge

We were out in the playground during recess. Me and Ryan and Michael all agreed that Ms. Hannah was weird. I mean, saving all that garbage is good for the environment and all, but it's kind of weird, too. She doesn't have enough garbage of her own. She has to go get *other* people's garbage.

"She's not an art teacher," I said. "She's a garbage collector."

"I still say our real art teacher was kid-napped," Ryan said. "She's probably tied up to a chair in the teachers' lounge."

The teachers' lounge is on the second floor of our school. Ryan said he thought it was in a room over the playground. We looked up at the windows and found the one that was probably the teachers' lounge.

"Our real art teacher could be in there right now," Ryan said, "tied up to a chair and being tortured!"

"Too bad we're too short to see inside," Michael said.

That's when I came up with the most genius idea in the history of the world.

I told Ryan and Michael that we might be able to see inside the window to the teachers' lounge if we stood on top of each other.

Michael got down on his hands and knees below the window. Ryan climbed up on top of him and hunched down. I climbed up on top of Ryan and stood on his shoulders.

"Can you see anything, A.J.?" Michael grunted.

"Not yet."

I could almost see into the window. I grabbed hold of the ledge on the window to pull myself up better.

"Hurry up!" Michael said. "My back is going to break!"

That's when I saw them. The teachers! I saw Miss Daisy and Mrs. Roopy and a few of the other teachers. I was looking right into the teachers' top-secret lounge!

"I see them!" I shouted.

"What are they doing?" Ryan asked, all excited.

"Not much," I said.

"Is anybody tied up to a chair?" Michael asked.

"No."

"Are they dancing around with each other?" Ryan asked.

"No."

"Are they playing Pin the Tail on the

Donkey?" Michael asked.

"No," I said. "They're just sitting there . . . eating lunch."

"That's *it*?" Ryan said.

"Wait!" I told them. "Mrs. Roopy is getting something out of the closet!"

"Is it a BB gun?" Michael asked.

"No, it's a paper bag," I said. "It must be her lunch."

"This is boring," Ryan said.

"One more minute," I said.

"My back is breaking!" Michael hollered.

I don't know exactly what happened next, but all I knew was that Ryan and Michael weren't holding me up anymore. *Nothing* was holding me up anymore.

40

I was holding on to the ledge of the windowsill with my elbows. If I let go, I would fall. I was afraid my head would bang on the windowsill.

"Help! Help!" I shouted.

I was hanging there for about a million hundred minutes until some of the teachers inside the teachers' lounge noticed me. They rushed over and opened the window.

"A.J., what are you doing out here?" Miss Daisy said as she and the other teachers pulled me inside.

"Uh, I was just hanging around," I told them.

The Museum of Hanging Garbage

For a few days, I was the star of the school. No kid had *ever* been inside the teachers' lounge. I was probably the first one in the history of the world.

Everybody wanted to know about the incredible things I saw in the teachers' lounge. Kids were even offering me candy to tell them.

I didn't want to tell them the teachers' lounge was just a boring old room where the teachers sat around eating lunch. I didn't want to lie, either. So I just told them that the teachers blindfolded me and said they would torture me if I ever revealed what went on in the teachers' lounge. It was cool.

Our next art class wasn't an art class at all. Ms. Hannah took us on a field trip to a museum.

I hate museums. Museums are boring.

"Why don't we ever take a field trip to a cool place like a skateboard park?" I asked Ryan on the bus ride over to the museum.

"What's so great about skateboard parks?" Andrea asked from the seat in front of me.

"Well, for one thing, *you're* not there," I said. Ryan laughed.

Andrea made a mean face at me. "I like museums," she said. "My mom takes me to museums all the time."

"Too bad she doesn't leave you there," I said.

Ryan laughed.

We walked around the museum for about a million hundred hours. Ms. Hannah was all excited. She just about ran from room to room telling us about all the wonderful art.

It was horrible and boring, and I was hungry and my legs were tired. I looked for a place to sit down.

There were some big boxes of soup cans in the corner, and I went to take a rest on them. But as soon as I sat down, all these loud bells started ringing and guards came running over. One of them was blowing a whistle, and he started yelling at me.

"Get up!" he shouted. "You can't sit there!"

"Okay, okay!" I said, getting up fast. "I'll sit someplace else." What's the big deal? I wondered.

The guard looked like he was going to arrest me or something. Luckily Ms. Hannah ran over and rescued me. I asked her what I did, and she told me that I had sat on some art.

"That's art?" I asked. "I thought it was boxes of soup."

"It's *modern* art!" she said. "That is a famous sculpture that is worth millions of dollars."

It looked like soup boxes to me. Ms. Hannah told me to remember that art is everywhere, so I should be careful what I sat on. She put her arm around me and kept it there for the rest of the time we were in the museum.

We walked around and she kept pointing out the beautiful artwork all over the place.

"Look at this!" she kept saying. "Isn't it marvelous?"

We stopped in front of a painting. It was just a bunch of lines and squares and box shapes. It was really stupid.

"Isn't it wonderful?" Ms. Hannah said. "It's called 'Broadway Boogie Woogie.'"

"My little sister could paint that with her eyes closed," I said.

The next room didn't have any paintings on the walls at all. But all kinds of junk was hanging from the ceiling.

"Can anybody tell me what these are?" Ms. Hannah asked us.

"That must be the museum's garbage," I told her. "When my family goes camping, we hang our garbage from a tree so the bears and raccoons don't get it."

"They don't have bears and raccoons

in museums, dumbhead," Andrea said. "Those things are called mobiles."

"That's right, Andrea!" Ms. Hannah said, and Andrea stuck her tongue out at me. I hate her. "They are also called kinetic sculptures."

"What does that mean?" Emily asked.

"It means it comes from Connecticut," I told her.

"No, *kinetic* means 'movement,'" Ms. Hannah said. "The sculptures can move."

"Don't tell me *that's* art," I said, looking at one of those Connecticut things.

"Not only is this art," Ms. Hannah said, "it's a masterpiece!"

"Looks like hanging garbage to me," I

said. This museum was the weirdest museum in the history of museums. I was bored and hungry, and I wanted to sit down. Finally Ms. Hannah said we could go outside in the garden and have a snack.

"Before we leave the museum," she started, "does anybody have any questions?"

I raised my hand. "If all of the stuff in here is art, how do they know what to throw away as garbage?" I asked. "Do they ever throw the art away by accident and leave the garbage here? How do they know which is which?"

Everybody laughed even though I

didn't say anything funny. I never did find out how they threw their garbage away.

Performance Art

There's a garden in the back of the Museum of Hanging Garbage. We went out there, and Ms. Hannah gave out pretzels and punch to all of us. She said we could run around and burn off some energy.

We were munching the pretzels when

Michael noticed a statue at the other end of the garden. It was a statue of a guy. He was dressed in a raincoat and he was holding an umbrella. The cool thing was that the statue guy was painted gold from head to toe.

"Now *that* is cool," I said.

A bunch of people were standing around in a circle looking at the statue guy.

"Hey, wait a minute!" Michael said. "I just saw that statue guy move."

"He did not," I said.

"Did too," said Michael.

I went over to the statue guy. There was a hat on the ground in front of him, and there was money in it. That was weird. If it was a statue, why would anybody give it money?

The statue guy wasn't moving at all. I walked around him real slow. I said "Boo!" to him. He didn't move. I wanted to touch him to see if he was a real statue, but I was scared.

I looked in the statue guy's eyes. They sure looked real, but he wasn't moving a muscle.

"See, I told you," I said to Michael. "It's just a stat—"

But just as I said it, the statue guy suddenly picked up his hand and put it on my head!

I screamed and jumped about three feet in the air! All the people who were watching started to laugh even though there wasn't anything funny about it.

I hadn't been so scared since I went to this haunted mansion on Halloween and

all these zombies were jumping out from behind the walls. When that statue guy moved, I thought I was going to die.

Ms. Hannah came over and put her arm around me.

"See, that's art too, A.J.!" she said as she put some money in the statue guy's hat. "This man has turned himself into a work of art! It's just like I always tell you. Art is everywhere. This is called performance art!"

Performance art? Performance art? I think maybe when I grow up, I will paint myself gold and stand around doing nothing but scaring kids all day. That performance art stuff is cool.

The Friendship Picture

When we got back to school, Ms. Hannah took us to the art room. What a mess!

There was more junk than ever in there. Her newspaper ball was bigger too. It was almost as tall as me.

Ms. Hannah said she hoped the art we saw in the museum had inspired us to create art on our own. She passed out paper and pencils and said that today we were going to draw friendship pictures.

"What's a friendship picture?" Emily asked.

"A friendship picture is a picture that two people draw together," she said.

"That sounds like fun," said Andrea. "Can Emily and I work on a friendship picture together? We're best friends."

"Can I draw a picture with A.J.?" asked Ryan.

"No," said Ms. Hannah. "I want Andrea and A.J. to work on a friendship picture together."

Everybody laughed even though Ms.

Hannah didn't say anything funny. That's because everybody knows that Andrea and I hate each other.

"Do I have to work with *him*?" Andrea asked.

"Do I have to work with *her*?" I asked.

"Yes," said Ms. Hannah. "Andrea, you love butterflies, right? A.J., you love skateboards. Let's see the two of you draw a skateboarding butterfly."

We got to work. Andrea drew the butterfly and the background. I drew a helmet on the butterfly, a skateboard under it, and a bunch of ramps and stuff.

Our friendship picture actually came out pretty good. Ms. Hannah was so impressed at how well me and Andrea worked together that she went to get Miss Daisy.

"Hey, this is pretty cool," I said, holding up our friendship picture.

"Wow," agreed Andrea, taking the friendship picture. "I'm going to take this home so my mom can put it up on the refrigerator."

"I want to take it home," I said, grabbing the friendship picture away from Andrea. "My mom will want to put it up on *our* refrigerator."

"You hate art, A.J.," Andrea said, grabbing the friendship picture back. "Why should *you* get to take it home?"

"Because I want it, that's why," I said. I grabbed the friendship picture back from Andrea. Only this time Andrea didn't let go.

She pulled on one side of the friend-ship picture. I pulled on the other side of the friendship picture. That's when our

friendship picture ripped right down the middle.

"You ruined our friendship picture!" Andrea shouted.

"I did not! You did!"

"I hate you!"

"I hate you back!"

I heard Ms. Hannah and Miss Daisy coming down the hall toward the art room.

"Wait until you see how well A.J. and Andrea are working together," Ms. Hannah said as they walked into the room. "You won't believe your eyes."

Mr. Klutz and the Secret Drawer

"You two," Miss Daisy said. "Go to Mr. Klutz's office. Now."

"Ooooooooooooooh!"

I thought Andrea was going to kill me on the way to the principal's office. She was really mad. Andrea had never been to Mr. Klutz's office before. That's because she never does anything wrong.

"I can't believe I'm in trouble," Andrea said. "It's all your fault, A.J."

"Relax," I said. "I've been to the principal's office plenty of times. Mr. Klutz is a good guy."

Mr. Klutz was sitting at his desk talking on the phone when we arrived. He is not only the principal of the school, but he also has no hair at all.

Once he let everybody in our class touch his head. It was cool.

"Are we going to be punished?" Andrea asked when Mr. Klutz hung up the phone. She was all nervous and talked in a quiet voice.

"I don't believe in punishing children," Mr. Klutz said. "I believe in rewarding children for doing good things. Now tell me, why can't you two get along?"

"He says mean things to me," Andrea said.

"She thinks she knows everything," I said.

"He hates everything."

"Not everything. Just you."

Mr. Klutz leaned forward in his chair and rubbed his forehead. Grown-ups always rub their foreheads when they are thinking. I guess it must help their brains work better. When you get old, your brain doesn't work as good anymore so you have to rub your forehead to get it going again.

"What can we do to solve this problem?" Mr. Klutz asked.

"Kick A.J. out of school."

"Kick Andrea out of school."

"I'm not kicking *anyone* out of school," Mr. Klutz said. "The two of you are going to have to live with each other."

"In the same house?" I asked. "I thought you said you don't punish kids."

Mr. Klutz laughed even though I didn't say anything funny. Then he took a key and opened one of his desk drawers. The drawer was filled all the way up to the top with candy. Chocolates. Lollipops.

Caramels. He had like a whole candy shop in his drawer. I decided right there that I want to be a principal when I grow up.

"Would you like some of this?" Mr. Klutz asked us.

Andrea and I nodded our heads and licked our lips.

"Here's the deal. If you two can go a full day without fighting, I will give you each a candy bar tomorrow."

"How about two candy bars?" I suggested.

"One candy bar each," Mr. Klutz said. "That's my final offer. Take it or leave it."

I don't like Andrea. She doesn't like me either. But we both like candy bars.

I would have to go one day without fighting with Andrea. One day wasn't so long. I could handle one day.

"Okay," Andrea and I said.

Then we all shook on it. Shook hands, I mean. We didn't just start shaking.

That would have been dumb.

10

The Big Stupid Art Contest

The next morning I was on my best behavior. I was trying very hard to not say anything mean to Andrea.

But it wasn't easy, because she is so annoying. When Andrea gave an apple to Miss Daisy as a present, I wanted to say something mean. But I didn't.

When Andrea showed everybody the A+ she got on the math quiz, I wanted to say something mean. But I didn't.

When Andrea told Miss Daisy how pretty her hair looked, I wanted to say something mean. But I didn't.

Andrea wasn't saying anything mean to me either. We both wanted that candy bar.

Miss Daisy was happy that Andrea and I were being so nice to each other.

When it came time for lunch, she sat us at the same table with Ryan and Michael and Emily. I traded Emily my banana, and she traded me her potato chips.

"Did you all bring in your stuff for the

art contest?" asked Emily. "Ms. Hannah is going to judge the winner this afternoon."

I had forgotten all about the stupid art contest. Michael said he made a statue out of toothpicks. Ryan said he made a papier-mâché head. Emily made a collage. Andrea made a mobile with hanging butterflies (of course!).

I was the only one who didn't bring in anything. I hate art. Art is stupid.

"Did you see the art room?" Andrea asked. "When I brought my mobile in, the place was just a big mess."

"Of course it's a big mess," Ryan said. "Have you ever seen Ms. Hannah throw anything away?"

"She can't throw anything away," Michael said. "She doesn't have a garbage can."

"That's exactly what I mean," Andrea said. "Ms. Hannah just gets more and more stuff, and never throws anything away. My mother is a psychologist. She helps people with their problems. And my mother says that people who can't throw anything away have a problem."

I was going to tell Andrea that *she* was the one who had a problem. But I didn't. I wanted that candy bar.

"You know, everything *isn't* art," Andrea said. "Some things are garbage. Maybe Ms. Hannah became an art teacher because she couldn't throw anything away. She might be a sick, sick woman who needs help."

"I never thought of it that way," Ryan said.

"We've got to help her!" said Emily.

"What can we do?" asked Michael.

"I've got an idea!" said Emily. "Why don't we sneak into the art room during recess and clean it up? When Ms. Hannah sees how neat and clean everything is, she will realize she has a problem."

"That's a great idea!" Andrea said.

It didn't sound like such a great idea to me. Cleaning things up was no fun at all. I don't like cleaning my room at home. I sure didn't want to clean up the art room. But I didn't want to get into an argument with Andrea either. If we had a fight, I wouldn't get my candy bar.

After we finished lunch, the five of us snuck down the hall to the art room.

Andrea was right. The place was a big mess. That's when I came up with the greatest idea in the history of the world.

"You know what?" I said. "Instead of

cleaning this place, we should mess it up even worse."

"Why would you want to do that?" Emily asked.

"If we really mess it up bad, Ms. Hannah will be so shocked that she will realize she has a problem."

It sounded like a genius idea to me. Cleaning isn't fun at all, but messing things up is lots of fun.

"I'm not sure that's such a good idea, A.J.," Andrea said.

"Sure it's a good idea," I said.

"Trust me, A.J. It's not a good idea."

Andrea thinks she knows everything. Well, she doesn't know everything.

"I'm not cleaning this place up," I said. "I'd rather go outside for recess."

"You promised you would help," Andrea said.

"I did not."

"Did too."

"I hate you, A.J.!"

That's when Andrea did the dumbest thing in the history of the world. She pushed me.

If I knew she was going to do something dumb like that, I could have gotten ready for it. But how was I to know she was going to do something dumb like push me?

My foot must have slipped or

something, because I fell backward.

Right behind me was Ms. Hannah's newspaper ball. When I fell backward, I landed on top of the ball.

The ball rolled. I rolled on top of it.

"Watch out!" Emily screamed.

My foot hit Andrea's butterfly mobile that was hanging from the ceiling. The butterfly mobile landed on my head.

On the floor behind the ball were a bunch of cans of paint. I tried to get out of the way, but I couldn't. When I hit the ground, I hit the paint first.

"You stupid dumbhead!" Andrea shouted. "You crushed my butterflies!"

"You pushed me into them!"

"I did not! You fell on them on purpose!"

I got up off the floor. Paint and butterflies were all over me. Red. Yellow. Blue. Green. It was cool.

"Hey, look!" I said. "Art is everywhere." Ryan and Michael laughed.

"How can you make jokes at a time like this?" Andrea said. "You ruined my mobile! Now I won't win the contest!"

"You're going to be in big trouble, A.J.," Emily said.

"Somebody's coming," Ryan said.

"Everybody shut up!"

That's when the door opened. Ms. Hannah and Mr. Klutz came in. I was standing there with paint and Andrea's stupid butterflies hanging all over me.

"What's the meaning of this?" Mr. Klutz asked. I didn't know what to do. I didn't know what to say. I had to think fast.

"It's . . . performance art," I said.

Everybody looked at me for like a million hundred seconds.

"Yeah," Andrea finally said. "It's *friendship* performance art. A.J. and I made it together."

Ms. Hannah walked around me and looked me over. One of the butterflies slid down my head and stopped at the end of my nose.

"It's Connecticut friendship performance art," I said.

"I think it's fabulous!" Ms. Hannah said. "It is so very creative. I believe the winners of the art contest are Andrea and A.J.!"

Everybody cheered and clapped. Mr. Klutz reached into his jacket pocket and pulled out two candy bars.

"I'm so pleased to see the two of you are getting along so well together," he said. "I promised you each a little something if you could go a day without fighting. Here is your prize. Congratulations!"

The candy bar tasted great. Maybe art isn't so stupid after all.

After it was all over, I still hated Andrea. Andrea still hated me. Ms. Hannah still had a big problem with collecting garbage. I said I would try to be nice to Andrea. She said she would try to be nice to me. And we both said we would try to help Ms. Hannah with her problem.

But it won't be easy!